Loving the Wrong Thug 3

By: Kia Meche'

Dedications:

Each book is dedicated to my baby boy, Aston, you give mommy the motivation to do this. I love you son and mommy got you.

Acknowledgements:

Once again I am back. First and foremost, I want to thank God because without him I would have never had the talent to write. I thank him so much for guidance and exploring my many talents.

I want to thank my mommy and sister for the support daily to keep following my dreams.

I want to thank my babe, Anthony, for motivating me and supporting me throughout this journey.

Thank you Tiara, Charae, and Jasmine for encouraging me on this journey.

Thank you to TMP, RWP, and KKP for rocking with me and Tiece for constantly believing in me.

Most importantly, my supporters all over, thank you so much for your constant support. I love y'all. #Nahforreal

Contact info:

Facebook: Kia Astonsmom Walton

IG: Meche_Aston

Sc: Astonmommy1226

My author page is Author Kia Meche

Other titles by me:

Lovin the Wrong Thug 1&2

Gotta Let it Burn

Hope you all enjoy. Once again thank you

One year later:
Chapter 1

Los:

It had been a year since Jas gave birth to little Demi and we were still going strong. Shit with her and that lame nigga Cody had been rocky because he had a problem with me being around his daughter. I understood it from a father's point of view, but I wasn't going nowhere and he needed to suck that shit up. She had finally given a nigga that sweet stuff and a nigga had been stuck. I'll admit; she had a nigga head gone.

"Ooh fuck daddy, just like that, don't move!" I was devouring the pussy like tomorrow didn't exist. I had her legs shaking and my toes were curling so hard, you could hear them bitches popping. "Circles baby circles, got damn you about to make this pussy cum!" She gyrated her hips against my face in a steady, yet slow motion. I had one finger in her pussy and my thumb in her ass. The shit was tasting so good; I could have cried. I fingered and thumb fucked her ass hard and fast, as I sucked forcefully on her pearl. Jas had the best tasting pussy you could ever taste. I sucked and slurped her dry until she barely had anything left. I slid the condom on my dick and rammed into her tunnel, showing her cat no mercy. I forcefully rammed my dick in and out as her juices saturated every inch of my dick.

"Yess, harder baby, fuck me harder." I wasted no time showing her the pain she begged and pleaded for. I was straight moaning like a bitch. She started scratching my back and trying to run, but I locked her legs into my arms.

"Where you going? Take this dick like I know you can." She started throwing it back just as hard as I was, matching my demanding thrusts. "My god, I'm about to cum." I took her breasts into my mouth, nibbling each one before I flipped her over until she was on all fours. Jas liked it rough and I loved that about her. She arched her back and tooted her ass as high as it would go. I swerved my dick in and out, hitting every wall her pussy possessed. "Shit girl." I started pumping faster as my dick stiffened and her juices came squirting mercifully. I filled the rubber with my babies as I pulled out. She tried to stand up and run to the bathroom but fell onto the floor.

"Damn boy. Swear, you got that dope dick. I will end up in jail fucking with you."

"Why you say that?"

"Give another bitch the dick and you will find out." Little did she know, I felt the same way about that million-dollar pussy between her legs. I see why that nigga Cody was dipping his hands in the cookie jar. She had something lethal. I had to get dressed because I had some business to take care of. I needed to holla at that nigga King about Marco. After careful consideration, I had decided he would have to let me in on getting this money or I planned on extorting his punk ass. Either way, I would get street justice for my cousin if I had to.

Rue:

Cali still wasn't talking to a nigga and it was damn near a year later. Thanks to Porsche and her big fucking mouth, Cali knew the biggest secret that I never intended on her finding out. I had never really planned on telling her about her thot ass sister because nothing ever happened. Nobody takes thots seriously, so she had to have known I would never fuck Chasity. Hell, any other woman, for that matter. I had been calling and texting her, trying to work shit out, but had yet to get a response. She was too damn stubborn to even hear a nigga out. I loved the hell out of Cali, but the fact that she felt like I left her hanging bothered me. I would never turn my back on her. She had been riding with a nigga more than anybody in my entire life and I appreciated her for that. It wasn't many bitches out here that would take a charge for a nigga but mines did. Chasity had still been calling my phone non-stop all week and I was tired of this hoe. It was bad enough her sister wasn't fucking with me, so I was not trying to add fuel to the fire by even holding a conversation with her.

"What man, damn?"

"So, your little girlfriend gets out and you act funny?"

"I don't talk to your ass like that shawty; why you tripping? Didn't I tell your simple ass to leave me the fuck alone?"

"Shit, Cali said y'all not together anymore, so what's the problem?"

"I don't give a damn Chasity. I still ain't fucking with you." I hung up the phone and called Sprint to change my number. Chasity was checking heavy for a nigga and I had never even touched the pussy. I needed to talk to Cali asap and I wasn't waiting for her to come to her senses any longer. I hopped in my Black Bentley Coupe and sped all the way to her house. I didn't even understand why she was trying me like I was some lame nigga. I pulled in next to her car and got out. After knocking for ten minutes, Mama Joyce finally answered as she was leaving out and told me Cali was in the shower. Letting myself into her room, I sat on her bed and waited for her to get out. She walked in and rolled her eyes.

"Nyrue, why are you here and, furthermore, why are you in my room?"

"So, you haven't been seeing a nigga calling your phone Calz?"

"Yeah, I saw it and I ignored it, so what you need? Now all of a sudden you want to talk but when I was down and out, I couldn't get at you. Fuck that! If you don't mind, I have things to do."

Chasity walked in without knocking and winked at me. Shawty was really on some disrespectful shit.

"The proper etiquette is to knock before you enter people shit."

Chasity laughed at Cali and waved her off. "Girl bye, nobody is worried about your lame ass. I came to get something that belongs to me."

"Nothing in here belongs to you, now, exit please."

She smirked at me. "Oh, Rue, you didn't tell her?" Calz was about to flip.

Dior:

It had been a year since everything went left in my life. After Adore tried to kill me, I was in the hospital for a little over a month. I heard that she was killed and I knew my fiancé had every bit of something do with it, even though he kept denying it. I had recently given birth to my baby boy and things were getting better for me. Me and King were now the parents of 2 boys and a girl. Christian, Cayleigh, and Carson. I wanted him to be a Jr. Dakota was coming over so that we could lay everything on the table. We had a wedding coming up and I didn't need any ill feelings around me. I was finally released from the hospital and I ended up finding out that I was pregnant. I just hoped that these two fools were on their best behavior because I didn't have time for the bullshit. Cody text and told me that he would be here in twenty, so I was trying to hurry and get dinner ready.

"He is on his way babe."

"Aight Dior."

"Chance, don't act like that. I wish the two of you would chill. Y'all have been doing good lately, but I need y'all to get better because he will be in the wedding."

"I guess. I'll be down in the basement; call me when he gets here." I had dinner all prepped and ready when Cody rang the doorbell. "Hey bro."

"What's good sis?"

"Nothing much. CHANCE COME ON!" By the look on Dakota's face, I could tell that this wasn't where he wanted to be. We all sat around the table and I started talking.

"As you both know, we are here to hash out any old feelings. Yes, I know that you two have been more than cordial, yet I want it to be better than that. You two are the most important men in my life and I love you more than anything. I am so happy that Cody will be in my wedding, but it doesn't feel right because he talks to me with all the arrangements. He is your groomsman, so he should be able to communicate with you. If you two love me, y'all would at least try to get closer."

Chance nodded his head. "She's right. We both will have major roles in her life, so it's only right we make this shit right for not only her but our kids."

"Facts. It's all love fam." They dapped each other up as they fixed their plates. I was so happy that went well. I didn't know how much more I could take.

****
***

My wedding was in less than two weeks and I was excited. Things with Chance and Cody were also slowly progressing, but I knew the smallest thing could set them back into war mode.

"Bae, where you put that bag with my clothes in it?"

"What bag? I didn't have a bag with your clothes." He was always losing something, then blaming me for it.

7

"The Ralph Lauren bag I brought home the other day Dior, damn."

"Wait a minute; kill the attitude. How the hell you going to get mad with me about something you lost? Explain that please."

He rambled on about the damn bag for almost twenty minutes before he found it. It was in the exact place that he left it. I finally planned on talking to my brother about the night our dad came to the hospital. That night brought back memories that I never wanted to relive. I just had to find the right way to come out and tell him because I knew Dakota was going to flip. I was getting the kids dressed so that we could attend our play date with my niece and nephews. Yes, you read that right. I am meeting up with Bree and Jasmine. After months of bickering between the two, I finally had them on the same page. Bree still felt like Jas and Dakota were messing around, but that was far from the truth. I pulled up to the park and Bree was out there with Demarri and Deimo. My nephews were one and bad as hell. I loved them like no other though.

"Hey chick, how are y'all?"

"Tired as hell honey. Your lazy ass brother working my damn nerves, like always." Who would have ever thought Cody would settle down and with Bree at that. I just knew he would always be that same thot ass nigga. My brother was really growing up for the most part though.

Bree:

I haven't been doing too much of nothing y'all, just cooling it. I had spent the past few months trying to cope with the loss of my sister. I missed Adore so much, it was ridiculous, but every action had a consequence. When I found out she tried to kill Dior, I knew her time on earth was limited. I had more common sense than they thought and I knew King was behind my sister's murder. I also knew that if King didn't get to her first, then Dakota would. I just wished I could have warned her and got her out of Atlanta before shit hit the fan. I hated that she let herself slip and fall in love with somebody that would have never belonged to her. I was just happy nobody placed blame of her actions on me and everything remained the same. Jasmine and I finally set our differences aside for the sake of the kids and had been getting along just fine. Every other week, I would meet up with her and Dior for a play date to keep the kids interactive with one another. Demarri and Deimo loved their little sister and didn't play the bar when it came to her.

"Hey y'all, sorry I'm late. I got off a little late." Dakota had told me that he and Jas had come to an agreement that she would take care of herself, so she ended up getting a job. She was working at Emory Hospital as a LPN. Even though we had our differences and weren't the best of friends, I would never take away the fact that she was a great mother. He still felt some type of way about Jas having her boyfriend around Demi, but I seriously doubt that he would place harm upon her. I had grown to love that little girl as if she was my own.

"You alright honey. Dior's ass wasn't on time her damn self."

"Damn bih, put me on blast then. I had to get some of that good good from daddy."

"Bitch, that is TMI." She stayed telling us about her sex life when I was the furthest from interested. The kids played for hours while we watched and talked until the sun started to set.

"Well, y'all, I have to get home and put my pots and pans to work. Dakota's greedy ass will come in the house bitching and I am not for it today." I put the boys and Demi in the car and pulled off. She always came over on the weekends, but I got her a day early. I called Dakota to see what he wanted for dinner.

I don't see how you deal with his ass. He is too damn spoiled Bree. You are better than me."

"Wait a minute; that is my twin y'all talking about."

"Exactly bitch, so you know exactly what the hell she talking about."

"Whatever bitches. We just love attention, that's all."

"Alright, see y'all next week." I got in the car and called Dakota. "Where you at?"

"Leaving the club, what's up?" He had recently opened up a club called Paradise, so he was always there. It brought in major bread, so I never nagged him about it, long as he continued to spoil me and keep me laced with the finest. I pulled up to the house and got the kids out. As soon as I got them situated, I started on dinner.

Chapter 2

Cody:

I had just touched back down in the city from Detroit. I went up north to kick shit and handle a lil business with my homie Murda. Life had been treating a nigga quite lovely these past few months. I had my princes and my princess, my fiancée, and my club. Me and Jas were even getting along. I had opened Club Paradise about four months ago and I was making good cash to the point I was barely in the streets. I was working extra hard so that I could leave the streets alone for good. I didn't want to continue getting my hands dirty when I had a whole family out here. Me and King had gotten better over time and he was alright, as long as he stayed in his lane. I wasn't trying to be the nigga best friend or no shit like that but since he was getting married to my sister, I knew I had to deal with him. The only problem I was left with was dealing with Jas' little boyfriend or whatever he was. She had the nigga cooped up in the house around my daughter and I didn't like that shit one bit. I was headed home with my family. I tried to make it home every night to spend time with my boys before bed. I was still a work in progress but, for the most part, I was happy. I had finally decided that I was serious about wanting to marry Bree and making shit official with us. It was nothing in these streets for me but sour pussy and death, so I was good where I was. I pulled up to the crib and got out. Walking into the house, the smell of fried pork chops invaded my nostrils.

One thing about my baby was she could cook her ass off. Bree could give Paula Dean a run for her money any day.

"What up Bree baby?" I walked over and gave her a kiss. Both of my boys ran over to me and I picked them both up. I hugged them tight then put them down. I grabbed Demi out of her car seat. I still couldn't believe I was somebody else's father and fiancé.

"You can get them cleaned up while I fix all the plates."

"Bet." I walked off, smacking her on the ass. We all sat at the table and ate dinner. After dinner, I helped her give the kids a bath and get them to bed, then hopped in the shower. Bree opened the shower and stepped in with me. She started stroking my dick and I let out a slight grunt.

"I want the pound game tonight daddy." That was all I needed to know before I pushed her against the wall. I grabbed one of her breasts and started nibbling on her nipple. While nibbling on her breasts, I slid two of my fingers in her pussy and started finger fucking her. "Mm. That feels so good." She lifted one of her legs so that my access was easier. Without wasting another minute, I rammed my dick into the golden gates. She started gyrating her hips in a circular motion with force. "Shit Cody, I'm cumin."

"Let that shit out bae." We were having a full blown fuck session in the shower. I slammed her back against the wall while beating the pussy like I was mad. "Argh. This pussy…" My words got caught in my throat as she squeezed my dick with her muscles. I picked her up, wet and all, and threw her on the bed. We fucked all night until the sun came up. I know for a fact she was pregnant again.

King:

The King is back and richer than a motherfucker. I was getting more money than I could count; not to mention, a nigga was about to be a married man. Me and Dior were getting married in less than two weeks and I was happy as fuck. I couldn't wait to make her my wife. She somehow convinced me to let her brother be in the fucking wedding and, to be honest, I hated that shit. Don't get me wrong; the beef between us had subsided but not to the point I wanted him in the wedding. I didn't mind him being there but damn, she had to push the issue. I would do anything for her though, so I obliged the idea. We hadn't bumped heads since that damn dinner she had last year. Killing Adore had still been fucking with me pretty tough. Every time I thought about my baby in that hospital, Adore's face would pop in my head. I didn't feel guilty about the shit though and I would do it all over again for my baby. Bree had been acting different towards a nigga, but I didn't have the slightest fuck to give. She should have warned her sister about a thoroughbred nigga like me. Moe had been getting Christian every other weekend and he was happy she was back. We had told him that they made a mistake with her death and she had gotten a job in another state. I refused to tell what really happened, since he was so young. The only thing left for us to do was finally tell her about being Dior's sister.

"What up nigga? What it's looking like?" I was getting a house built over in Princeton Lakes as a gift to Dior. It had six bedrooms and seven baths. I wanted more than enough space for all of the kids.

"We will be done with it in less than three months. I think wifey will love it."

"Facts my man. That's what's up; let me get out of here and handle a little business." I pulled off and headed to the warehouse to get ready for a new shipment. I had to meet up with my plug for a meeting he came up with at the last minute. I pulled up to the warehouse and got out. When I walked in, he was tying up a conversation with some nigga with dreads. It didn't hit me until he turned around and it was Cali's little boyfriend.

"Yo King, what's good my man? This is my son. King meet Rue, your new connect."

Jas:

My princess was about to be one next week and spoiled was an understatement. The day I held her in my arms was the most beautiful day of my life. Dakota and I were great at co-parenting, even though he hated Los being around. I never understood how niggas could have as many bitches that they wanted around but didn't want niggas around their kids. To me, that was such a double standard. Anytime he came to pick her up, he would start his bullshit. I always ignored his ass because he didn't run shit but his mouth. Things between me and Bree had even gotten better. I had heard they were engaged to be married but who knows. She had become a tad bit anti-social after her sister was killed but who wouldn't. I ride for Dior any day, so I would have ended up killing her but somebody beat me to it. I had somewhat a clue that King had done it, but it wasn't my business to ask. That bitch got what she deserved.

I had finally got on my grown woman and got a job. Even though I didn't make as near as Dakota blessed my account with, I got it on my own. Los kept my pockets fat also. Speaking of Los, I was getting dressed for our date night. Demi was at her father's house for the rest of the week. He made sure to take me out every Thursday and, on Saturdays, we watched movies. I hopped in the shower and bathed my body with Cucumber & Green Tea Dove body wash. I stayed in the shower until the water turned cold. I got out and put on a face mask until I got myself dressed. I applied vanilla oil all over my body from head to toe. I went into the closet and grabbed my BCBG Maxazria Bridette coordinate set with my Christian Louboutins. I had recently got some inches installed, so I flat ironed my 30-inch Brazilian bone straight with a side part. I washed off my face mask and beat my face to perfection. I applied all of my MAC products and sprayed my body with Coco Chanel fragrance and I was ready to go. I sent Los a text to see where he was.

WYA?

Bae: Be there in five.

I grabbed my Fendi clutch bag and went downstairs to wait for him. I did a once over in my full length mirror and was more than satisfied with my results. "Miss Jasmine, you are one bad bitch?

Don't I know it?" I was standing in the mirror having a full blown conversation with myself. Los knocked on the door and when I opened it, his entire ensemble and fragrance took my breath away. He had on a pair of khaki pants with a brown and tan Polo cardigan. His dreads were styled to perfection. His watch damn near blinded me and he had on a pair of Polo skippers. The Polo Black fragrance had my crotch soaked and twisted. If our plans were not reserved, he would have gotten the goodies right there at the front door. He grabbed my hand and we made our way out of the front door. When I walked around the corner, there was a bad ass old school Monte Carlo on 26-inch Asanti rims.

"Baby, whose car you done stole?"

"Stole? Girl, I'm gwopped the fuck up. I don't have to steal shit. This all me."

He threw me the keys and told me to drive. I felt like one of those boughetto bitches driving that hood ass car. I pulled the seat up and he started laughing.

"Yo, why you got the seat like that? You damn near in the steering wheel." He was always cracking jokes but, hell, I couldn't see shit.

"Shut up, I can't see over this damn steering wheel." We pulled off in route to our destination. Tonight, we were dining at the Red and Green Steak House. Our reservations weren't for another hour but traffic was always bad going towards Buford Hwy. I hopped on the e-way and cruised on 75. He lit a blunt and pulled three times, then passed it to me. The aroma was pure pleasure to my nostrils as I inhaled the pressure that would bless my lungs. We pulled up to the restaurant and I was high as a giraffe's pussy. I wasn't a heavy smoker until I started dealing with Carlos. He was a real life stoner. He put me up on numerous kinds of weed since he had me by at least ten years. We were seated at our table and I started looking over the menu.

"You treating tonight, right? I left my wallet at the house."

"Is that so? Well, I'm pretty sure they need help in the kitchen." We both started laughing as the waitress approached our table to take our orders.

"Yes, I will have a Passion Fruit juice and he will have a Bud Light. For our entrees, I will have the Filet Mignon with bacon."

"And I will have the Rump steak."

The waitress left to put in our orders and we started chatting a little.

"So baby, how was your day?"

"It was alright. I met up with the girls and that's about it. How was yours?"

"Everything was good until my dumb ass baby mama called with her bullshit. She so fucking messy; I don't see how I was involved with a bitch that ratchet." Swear, I couldn't wait to see what his baby mama looked like. The way he talked about her, I knew she was one of those dumb dust rats that stayed causing chaos because their baby daddy didn't want them. It really didn't bother me though, as long as she didn't come for me. Our food arrived and we were silent as we ate. I ate every ounce of my meal, thanks to having the munchies. He paid the tab and we headed to my house. I couldn't even get in the house before Los started attacking me. We made love all night until the sun arose.

Chapter 3

Cali:

I had been staying under the radar, allowing my heart to heal from the pain Nyrue caused me. I couldn't believe he thought that everything would be all good, considering the fact that he basically gave me his ass to kiss during my entire bid. Not only that, but his crackhead looking ass cousin put me up on game about him and my sister. True enough, he didn't take it to the next level with her but to keep the shit from me was just as bad. I had not talked to him in over two months and didn't plan on it. I was in the shower enjoying the relaxation that the hot water delivered to my body when I heard somebody in my room. I stepped out of the shower and wrapped my towel around me. When I stepped into my room, Nyrue was sitting on my bed, as if he belonged.

"Nyrue, why are you here and, furthermore, why are you in my room?"

"So, you haven't been seeing a nigga calling your phone Cali?"

"Yeah, I been seeing it and I ignored each one, so what you need? Now all of a sudden you want to talk but when I was down and out, I couldn't get at you. Fuck that! No need to explain, so if you don't mind, I have things to do." I let the towel loose and started oiling down my body. I could see him staring out of my peripheral. He could look all he wanted but he sure better not touch.

Chasity walked in without knocking and she was really on some disrespectful shit.

"The proper etiquette is to knock before you enter people shit."

Chasity laughed and waved me off. "Girl bye, nobody is worried about your lame ass. I came to get something that belongs to me."

"Nothing in here belongs to you, now, exit please."

"Rue, you want to tell her or should I?"

She walked over to Nyrue and tried to sit on his lap, but he pushed her off.

"The fuck is you doing? Yo Cali, I didn't-" he was cut off because I had charged at the both of them. Before he could put his hands up to stop me, I was whooping Chasity's ass. I was delivering blow after blow and Chasity was no match. Chasity somehow got ahold of my hair and slung me into the dresser, breaking the mirror. I grabbed a piece of glass and sliced Chasity across the face. He grabbed at me and I sliced him on the arm.

"Both of y'all get the fuck out before I end up back in jail. I don't know why you brought your stupid ass over here in the first place. Chasity, you are dead to me. I won't lie; you are pretty as hell, but you are too jealous hearted and I don't rock with jealous bitches." Chasity ran out of the room crying with blood leaking all over the floors.

"Why the fuck you cut me? I ain't do shit; your sister came onto me. Baby, I'm sorry for leaving you by yourself in there but-" I cut his ass off. True enough, he was innocent at that moment, but I was too livid to give a fuck.

"Get out." I went into my closet and he ran out because he already knew I was about to get my gun. I was so hurt that my sister would dare hurt me like this. The way she was open to even try to sit on his lap showed me she never gave a damn about me so, for that, I would disown her. Lord knew how much I loved Nyrue, but forgiving him was the hardest thing for me to do right now. I was wrong in all aspects of the matter for cutting him the way I did. I will admit that he didn't deserve that. I threw on a pair of jogging pants and a white v-neck t-shirt. I put on my white Forces and went towards Chasity's room. I just wanted to know why she would try to hurt me like this. I walked down the hall and started beating on her door.

"Go away. I hate you."

"Tuh, don't I know it? Open the door so that we can talk." I was tired of people not giving a damn about me. I thought I had found the perfect man that cared, but he left me to fend for myself. After five minutes, she finally opened the door. I had really messed up her face and I felt bad. The cut that I granted her went from her eyebrow to her top lip, a few more inches and I could have cut her eye. It was still severely bleeding.

"I apologize for slicing you in the face, but I think you need stitches. Why would you try to hurt me like that Chasity?"

"I don't know, ok. Maybe you were right; I am jealous of you. Ever since we were younger, you have always gotten all of the attention. You are so pretty and have those gorgeous eyes; I have to wear contacts and niggas still don't pay attention. I sleep with random niggas hoping that I will find the one and you have a nigga that worships the ground you walk on. He takes great care of you and I guess I just thought he would do the same for me. Everybody knows me as 'Chas that gives up the ass'; do you know how that feels? Of course not." Even though I hated her at that moment, I still sympathized with her. I was so caught up that I didn't notice she had a packed suitcase on the bed.

"Where are you going?"

"I just need to get away Cali. I need to be alone for a while." With that being said, she grabbed her bag and I moved out of her way. True enough, my intentions walking in was to beat her ass again, but a part of me understood her reasoning.

Rue:

It literally took everything in me, including a prayer, not to beat the shit out of Cali. She had lost every piece of her mind when she cut me. That usually meant a motherfucker wanted to die, but she was lucky I loved her. I didn't understand why the fuck her anger was so intense with me in the first place but that's a woman for you. Chasity had somehow gotten my new number and had been calling my phone over and over since I pulled off.

"What man, damn? Why the fuck you keep blowing a nigga phone up?"

"I'm on the way to the hospital. I think I need stitches; can you please meet me there?"

"Meet you for what? Nah ma, I'm not fucking with you. We both just got sliced the fuck up back there or did you forget?" I hung up the phone and turned up the music. I didn't have time to be dealing with Chasity and her bullshit. She was going to literally be the death of me. I was headed to meet up with my pops to talk about this situation with King. He had just touched down and told me to meet him at his old warehouse. I was listening to Kevin Gates "2 Phones" single and cruising.

I got two phones, one for the plug and one for the load
I got two phones, one for the bitches and one for the dough
Think I need two more, line bumpin' I'm ring, ring, ringin'

I pulled up to the warehouse and grabbed the blunt from behind my ear. I lit it as I walked in to greet my father. He told me that King would be headed that way and to let him do all the talking. We were mapping out a new plan since he was stepping down and I was taking over. I couldn't wait to see this nigga's face when he found out I would be his new connect. I finished smoking my blunt while my pops finished discussing how he wanted me to run things. King walked in and my father introduced us, "Yo King, what's good my man? This is my son. King meet Rue, your new connect."

King:

"New connect? What the fuck is going on here?" I went from 0 to 100 real quick. There wasn't no way in hell I would be taking orders from this young ass nigga. Shit was not good between me and him because he was the same nigga that was fucking my sister.

"I am stepping down; he will be taking over and supplying you. No need to worry because your prices are set."

"I don't know about this shit man. You could have been told me this shit and I could have weighed my options. Now, you putting me in a bind. I will see how this shit works out man but this shit doesn't sit right with me. You know how I roll and I don't like too many new niggas around me." I didn't give a fuck how neither of them felt because at the end of the day, it was my cash being spent.

"Nyrue will take care of everything and I promise you will not have any problems. I am happy to see you two are all about the money. I know what's going on between you two but let's get paid; fuck all the small talk. If it is going to be a problem, then I will get rid of you both. I don't need you two to let your little feelings get in the way of my money."

"Nah pops, I'm good." He looked at me for confirmation that I was good also.

"Everything all good." We all sat down and discussed what new products I would be distributing. Since this was a new product, he discounted it to see how it would sell. I knew now that I was about to make some major bread. We tied everything up and I headed home to my family. I stopped by the florist and got my baby a dozen different color roses. Since I had been doing around the clock work, I had not been home much, but she didn't nag me about it. I called Moe to set up a meeting with the two of them.

"Hey baby daddy, to what do I owe this phone call?"

"What's up Moe? Pull up at the house, wifey wants to holla at you."

"Oh Lord, what I done did now? You know she crazy, right?"

I started laughing because I couldn't agree with her more. "Nah, it's a serious type of conversation. I will be there in twenty." Moe had really stepped up when it came to taking care of Christian. I would never keep her from him because I knew how much he loved his biological mother. His birthday was next month and a nigga was going all out for it. I pulled up to the house and Moe was getting out of her house. A nigga couldn't even flex and lie like my baby mama wasn't bad. She was looking sexy as fuck in those jean True Religion shorts. That ass had gotten fatter and she looked delicious.

"Umm, nigga don't burn a hole in me. I know I'm thicker than a snicker." I snapped out of the trance her body held me in and walked up to unlock my door. Dior and all of the kids were watching TV. She looked up and saw Moe standing beside me. The attitude was evident on her face.

"MOMMY!" Christian ran up and hugged her, and Dior walked towards the kitchen as I followed suit.

Chapter 4

Dior:

I had finally convinced Chance to get me and Moe together so that we could finally talk. I was sitting in the living room enjoying my kids when Chance and Moe walked in. It pissed me off because I didn't know he would bring her ass home with him. I planned on meeting her at a restaurant or somewhere public. Of course, he had to do the unthinkable. I walked towards the kitchen to keep myself sane. I knew he was following behind me, so I pulled myself together.

"Why I feel like you have an attitude?"

"I'm good babe. I just didn't know we would be meeting today but fuck it. Can you take the kids out for a while? I will behave."

He looked at me with a side-eye, but I was serious. There was no reason for me to prolong this issue any longer.

"Alright Dior, don't be on no fuck shit." He kissed me on the forehead and left the kitchen. I grabbed two bottles of water and walked back towards the living room and Moe was sitting on the couch.

"Water?" I handed her the bottle and sat down.

"So, what did you need to talk to me about?" She got straight to the point.

"I don't even know how to explain the shit I am about to tell you but whatever; let me just get straight to it. I recently found out that you happen to be my older sister. Our mother told me that she had given you up for adoption when you were just a baby. I know you probably didn't know and I was tired of holding it in. She was looking for you so that you all could bond but was told you were dead. You know, like we all thought?" I saw her fighting to keep the tears inside but failed miserably. I knew this was a touchy subject for anybody.

"What? Is this some type of joke? How is that possible? Where is she now?" She jumped up and she was livid.

"She is dead. Our mother was a hit woman and her life caught up with her. I'm sorry you have to find out this way. I also know you have many unanswered questions, but I don't really have the answers. What I do know is I wanted you to know so that we could get our lives in tact with one another. This is a crazy ass situation since we have kids with the same man but he is my man and long as you understand that, we are good." No words were spoken for the remainder of her visit. I knew the news she had just received was a bit much and I sympathized with her about it. The only thing we could do from here on out was move forward. She was an ok person, even though we had our moments of drama.

"Thank you Dior. We will talk but I have to go. This is too much right now." She got up and left without another word.

Moe:

28

When Chance told me that Dior wanted to talk to me, I did not expect the shit I had just heard. I was emotionally and mentally fucked up. All these years I had been without a family when I had siblings. It hurt me to the core that my mother gave me away, like I meant nothing to her. I went from foster home to foster dealing with men and women molesting me. Nobody knew what I went through, not even Chance. The only person I had ever told about my past was Adore, my therapist, but she was dead. I literally had nobody I could vent to. I knew Dior felt a little sorry for me, but I was just out of it right now. Chance started calling my phone and I answered.

"Yes?"

"What's up ma? I was just calling to check on you. You good?"

"What do you think? My question to you is how long have you known?"

"Ma, that wasn't my place to tell you that shit. She told me she would tell you, so I let her handle that. I didn't call for all that though. I was only seeing if you were good?"

"Well, I'm not." I hung up the phone before he could respond. I was all fucked up. Tears were pouring from my eyes like faucets. My heart literally hurt me. Why couldn't I have died instead of falling into a coma? I had nobody that would have missed me. Christian was better off without me. I was too broken. I just wanted to run away, but I knew that wasn't what was best right now. I knew without a doubt that my son loved me unconditionally. I also knew that I needed to apologize to Dior for leaving like that when she was only trying to make this right. I was completely wrong for placing blame on her for our mother's mistakes. Now that I knew she was my sister, I realized the similarities that we shared. This would take time, but I had to be an adult and pull it together. I was not going to let my past affect my present or my future any longer. My son was depending on me and I refused to let him down. I did a U in the middle of the street and headed back to Chance and Dior's place. I was going to embrace my little sister. I had missed out on enough of their life and I did not want to be the old selfish Monique.

Cody:

I had been calling Jasmine all morning so that I could take Demi home. I was getting pissed off because she wasn't answering. I had a very important meeting that I needed to get to.

"Why don't you just take her home since she's not answering?"

"Yo Bree, I don't need your suggestions right now. Just shut the fuck up and let me handle this."

"No sir, you won't. You better check that mouthpiece before my fist lands in it. I was just trying to help your sour ass; don't get mad with me." She was adding fuel to the fire and I wasn't in the mood for it. I grabbed Demi and her bag and headed out. I strapped her in her seat and pulled off. Jas' ole thot ass better not have been ignoring my calls for some dick. I already didn't like her little gremlin looking ass boyfriend around my baby and she was pushing it. It took me about twenty minutes to get to her house and, luckily, she was home. I got my baby out of the car and started beating on her door. I didn't give a fuck that her nosey ass neighbors had come outside.

"Take y'all punk asses back in the house. Ain't shit going on over here." She swung the door open with a mean scowl plastered on her face.

"Aye man, why the fuck your baldhead ass not answering the phone? I got shit to do and you probably in here busting it open for a pussy nigga."

"Whatever Dakota, you mad or nah? Give me my damn baby and go on about your business." I handed Demi over and got back in my car. I didn't have time to argue with her dumb ass. I don't know why I allowed her to piss me off the way she did. I guess her situation with that nigga slick bothered me more than I would like to admit. Call a nigga selfish, but a part of me didn't want her to move on. I pulled off and headed to The Georgian Terrace. I stopped by the gas station before my shit broke down. I was standing in line paying for my gas when I felt a light tap on my shoulder.

"Simone, what's good?" Simone was this little thot I dealt with a couple of months ago. Our situation didn't get anywhere because her pussy was garbage juice. I never planned on seeing her again but look at Satan. He was being petty, making me run into this sad waste of a woman.

"Damn, you just stopped calling me huh? How have you been though?"

"After our last encounter, I figured you would have gotten the picture. No offense ma but you have no place in my life, so why even waste either of our time."

"Still the same rude ass Cody I see."

"Ain't nothing change baby but the time. I will see you around though. I got shit to handle." I left out of the store and damn near forgot to pump my gas. Some he-woman was sitting there mugging the shit out of me.

"The fuck you looking at lil boy?" She tried to turn her head and I got in my car. I didn't play the bar and would beat the nigga mentality out of it if need be. I pulled off and headed to take care of business.

Los:

"Aye ma, I'm getting real tired of your fake thug ass baby daddy. I won't keep sparing that nigga on the strength of you. Lil mama not going to have a daddy if he keeps on with the tongue twisting."

"Carlos, not right now, alright. I am so tired of the two of you and this backyard beef."

"Backyard beef? The fuck is that supposed to mean?"

"Backyard, meaning the beef is not known. I only know about it but y'all never say shit to each other. Leave me out of that shit." I could have knocked her fucking head off of her shoulder. I didn't deal with disrespect well and I felt she was trying me.

"What the fuck? That soft ass nigga has an issue with me and don't know shit about me."

"OK, if we are going to talk about Dakota all day, you can leave. I don't want to hear that shit."

"Say no more. I'm out."

I didn't have time for this bitch and her dumb ass baby daddy. I had bigger fish to fry, like coming up with a plan to get at King. I would deal with that situation with Cody later. I was sick of him and his mouth. He was just mad because I had his bitch. I headed to my car lot to make sure business was running smooth. It was too much money out here to be worried about the next nigga. I was a grown ass man and would not stoop to a child's level. I was ready to cause hell with them niggas, King and Cody. Before I laid either of them out, I planned on taking them for everything they had. I was ready to come out of retirement. He had woken up the beast in me. My phone started ringing and it was my slow ass baby mama.

"Hey hubby. I'm in the A."

"Chill out with that dumb shit. I am not your hubby and what the fuck you doing here? Aye, don't come here on no bullshit ma."

"Boy bye. I am not worried about your limp dick ass. Run me my money, that's what you do." She hung up before I could respond.

My baby mama was nothing but drama and I didn't have time for it. She never allowed me to move on and truly be happy since we didn't work out. I knew since she was here, there was about to be a lot of bullshit going on. "FUCK!"

Chapter 5

Bree:

I was sitting here having a conversation with Adore about life. I would have never guessed I would be sitting here talking to my sister's spirit. This was still all new to me and I missed her more than words could describe. As much as I tried to play happy, I was so broken. I had nobody I could go to for advice because the only person I had was dead and gone.

"I miss you so much sis. I wish I could turn back the hands of time. You left me out here all alone and I'm going crazy. The boys are getting bigger and I wish you had the chance to be an auntie to them." I didn't know I was crying until I felt wetness on my arms. King took away the most important thing I had left, besides my kids. I had yet to confront him about what I already knew, but his time was coming. He was just a typical nigga to get mad at the next motherfucker because he got caught up. I didn't want to be around a nigga like that, so I had been staying to myself. Something told me that Dakota had been back on his bullshit, but I had no solid proof. I would not tolerate that shit if I found out.

"Alright sis, I'm going to get out of here. I just had to stop by and see you. I love you, Adore, and I'm sorry for everything."

I got back in my car and pulled off. I was crying my eyes out, thinking about everything that had happened this past year. I was always the type to wear my sleeves on my shoulder, but I was tired of fronting like everything was all good. I wanted everybody that hurt me to pay for what they had done. I headed to pick the boys up from school and get dinner ready. I didn't feel like really cooking, so I was going to cook spaghetti since it was quick. After getting the boys and pulling up at home, I noticed Dakota wasn't home. This was his new routine lately. He was rarely home and I had grown tired of it. I barely received help with the boys and it was unfair. I called to see where he was.

"Where are you?"

"Damn, a hello would have been nice. I'm out."

"I see that much nigga. I asked where you at?"

"Aye, chill the fuck out Bree; what you doing all that for?"

"I am cooking dinner so bring your ass." I hung up before I said some shit I would regret. He had me fucked up if he thought I would continue to deal with the bullshit. He could have stayed with his other baby mama if that was the case. I put the boys to sleep and hopped in the shower. I stepped under the hot water and the tears started flowing freely. My mind, body, and soul was tired. I was in need of a serious break. The shower curtains snatched back and he stood there looking stupid.

"The fuck you standing in here crying for?"

"Dakota, just leave me alone." I got out of the shower and walked pass him. Talking to his ass was like talking to a brick wall and it was something I didn't feel like doing.

Cali:

It had been over a week since Chasity left. I had yet to talk to Nyrue and I wasn't in a rush to do so. True enough, I knew there would be a day that I would have to talk to him but, right now, it was fuck him. I heard the front door open and I went to see who it was. My mother came in and she was on the phone. She hung up and started going in on my ass. "What the fuck is Chasity telling me about you cut her? Have you lost your got damn mind, Cali Frazier? I should beat your ass fighting over that no good ass nigga. Y'all young bitches kill me fighting over dick like it's not plenty on earth."

"Damn, can I talk?" She cocked her head.

"Who the hell you cursing at?"

"You. You come in here talking that rah rah and that bitch you taking up for is the same bitch that tried to fuck my man. That shit is trifling on all levels and you sitting your childish ass here talking about her." She slapped the shit out of me and I fell.

"Get your ass up and get the fuck out of my house. I should send your simple ass to live with your daddy, but I forgot he don't even want your ass." She put her hands over her mouth, but she had already said too much.

"What did you just say Joyce? Don't stop talking now; tell that cat let go of your tongue. So, I don't have the same father as Chance and Chasity?"

She shook her head no and reached out to me, but I slapped her hands away.

"Don't you dare fucking touch me. How could you lie to me all my life? So, you an old thot?"

"Cali, let me explain please." I didn't want to hear shit she had to say. This was no mother of mines. I had a different father from my siblings and he didn't even want me.

"You foul for this shit. Did Chance know this?"

Silence.

"Answer me damn it. You had so much to say a few minutes ago."

I didn't even wait to hear another lie. I stormed to my room to pack some clothes. I refused to continue to be in this house full of ain't shit women. I got my suitcases and headed out the door. Before leaving, I went back into the kitchen. "And so there is no misunderstanding, you and Chasity are dead to me. I hate the both of you." I turned to leave.

"Cali, don't do this please. I am so sorry."

"Fuck you and your apology." I left out and vowed to never look back. As soon as I shut my door, I started crying non- stop. How could my mother keep such an important detail of my life away from me? I wanted to meet the nigga that gave me life and confront him. I didn't know where I was going but I had to get away. I stopped at Ruby Tuesday to sit down and map out my future. Everybody around me wanted to hurt me and I refused to let them break me. I walked in the restaurant and the sight before me pissed me off.

"What the fuck is this?"

"Cali, it's not what you think?" Nyrue and Chasity had me fucked up, and I was about to light this restaurant up.

Rue:

After the meeting with my pops and King, I went home to take a shower. When I hopped out, I had six missed calls and text from Chasity. She wanted to apologize to Cali about the shit that popped off at the crib. She had not seen nor talked to her sister since that day and she was feeling bad as fuck. She told me to meet her at Ruby Tuesday to help come up with a way to get Cali to forgive the both of us. A nigga really didn't understand why the fuck she was at me in the first place. I scooped up this little bitch named Mya that I met the other day and went to meet up with Chasity. Now, I know that shit sounds crazy since I am with Chasity's sister but, for the moment, I was just mingling a bit until she came to her senses. It wasn't like I was fucking the bitch. It was an innocent dinner. We were halfway into our meal when I heard a very familiar voice, "What the fuck is this?" I almost shitted on myself when I saw my baby standing there with the evilest scowl on her face. I could tell that she had been crying and that shit crushed my soul.

"Cali, it's not what you think?"

"So, this how you do? You sitting here wining and dining with two bomb bitches?" Mya stood up like she wanted a problem.

"Hold on now; whatever y'all have going on, leave me out of it. I am far from a bomb bitch." Cali mushed her ass in the face and she fell back into the booth. She snatched Chasity out of the booth and started beating her ass once again. I pulled her off and Mya jumped on my back. Now, I didn't know who this bitch thought she was, but I flung her ass into the table next to us while still holding on to Cali. Chasity jumped up and sucker punched Cali in the eye. It was like Cali became the Incredible Hulk the way she broke loose. She tried to charge at Cali again but was yanked up. When I looked up, it was their brother, King. I don't know where the fuck he came from but I was glad he showed up.

Mya got up and started talking shit, "You will regret this shit."

"Yeah, whatever bitch. Shut up. Walk your simple ass home."

King grabbed both of his sisters and pushed them towards the front door. I peeled off two hundreds and threw it on the table. I was embarrassed as fuck. I walked outside to where they were and King was going in on the both of them.

"What the fuck y'all doing fighting like some fucking hood rats? Then, fighting each other at that. Cali, what the fuck is your problem?"

"She's a dumb bitch, that's what's wrong. You see my fucking face? The bitch sliced me in the face."

"Fuck your face thot pocket. Your precious little sister has been trying to fuck Nyrue and I found out about it. Both of them trifling motherfuckers sitting in there having dinner like a couple and shit while I just found out some bullshit."

"I should beat the both of y'all asses. Chasity, why would you do some shit like that? Cali, that still doesn't give you the right to be acting stupid in public. I'm calling Joyce." He pulled out his phone and started calling their mother.

"Fuck Joyce. Did she tell you that I didn't have the same daddy as you and Chasity?"

He looked at her and hung up the phone. Chas stepped around King. "Wait, what? Don't tell lies on my mommy Cali, that shit is not cool."

"Aww, shut the hell up Chasity. The both of you bitches are one in the same. Two grade-a thots." Cali had started crying and I went to comfort her, but she pushed me. "Don't touch me." She turned to walk away and my heart was crushed. I was lost without my Calz. I had to do something to get her back. I hate that we had come to this and I refused to let her hate me. I apologized to King and Chasity and walked off. I got in my car and grabbed my blunt out of the ash tray. I was stressed the fuck out and needed to go to the moon for a while. I lit the blunt and pulled on it long and hard. I sat in the parking lot smoking my blunt until it was no longer existent and started my car. I called Cali, only to be sent to the voicemail. I sent her a text before I pulled off.

Baby I am so sorry that I keep fucking up. Please don't give up on me ma you are everything to me.

Calz: Sure (Sad face)

I would die before I let her give up on me. Cali was my heart and I couldn't let her go. I pulled off and headed home. I pulled up to the house and went inside. I laid in my bed and immediately fell asleep.

Chapter 6

Dior:

We had not heard from Moe since she came over. Chance had been trying to reach her, yet failed each time. It was pissing me off because Christian wanted to see her. I didn't give a damn about her being upset with me, but she could at least check on her son. My phone started ringing, drifting me from my thoughts.

"Hello!"

"Hello Dior, it's Moe."

"Monique, where are you? Christian has been asking for you." I didn't even care about how she got my number.

"I know and I apologize; I just had to clear my head. Please, don't use that against me. You have to understand where I'm coming from with my pain." I understood to the fullest the gratitude of the situation. I couldn't knock her for everything she went through.

"I understood. So, when will you be coming to get him?"

"Will it be alright if I come by tomorrow?"

"Sure, that will be fine. We will be home by 6:30."

"Thank you so much Dior."

"No problem Moe, and you can call me sis if you would like." I couldn't believe the words that had just exited my mouth. It was very true, though, and I would love nothing more than to build a bond with my older sister.

"Thank you so much." We hung up the phone as Chance walked thru the door. He walked over to me and kissed me on the forehead, but I could tell something was bothering him.

"Hey babe, what's wrong?"

"You wouldn't believe what I saw today. Both of my sisters were fighting like two bitches in the streets. The shit pissed me off to the point that I was about to beat the shit out of them both."

"Wait a minute; who were they fighting?"

"Each other. Bae, they were fighting like they didn't know each other. They were fighting over Cali's punk ass boyfriend. Then, to top that shit off, that nigga is going to be my new connect. I had a pretty fucked up day. What about you? Did Moe call you?"

"Yeah, I was wondering how the hell she got my number. She is supposed to come get Christian tomorrow around 7." I stood behind him and started massaging his shoulders. I hated when he seemed so tense. He turned around and started kissing me in such a forceful manner, yet it instantly made my pearl start throbbing. He picked me up and carried me up the stairs with my legs wrapped around his waist, steady kissing me. When we got into our bedroom, he threw me onto the bed and we both started undressing. He started kissing my body from head to toe as I let out a slight moan.

"Mm, baby that feels great." He slid my thong off and dived right in. I had gotten a Brazilian wax done, so my kitty was pretty and ready. He started feasting on my pussy as if he missed a few meals. My head rolled back as I held onto his. "Yes baby, right there." He started finger fucking me while sucking on my clit. I felt my body tensing up as his tongue waited patiently for my juices to grace it.

"Come on baby, feed your nigga." I did as I was told and gave him all of me. He slurped my pearl until there was nothing left. He came up and placed his lips on mines then fell beside me. "Sit on this dick."

I hopped on top of him and started bouncing up and down as if I had something to prove. He gripped my waist. "Fuck bae, slow down." I ignored him and started grinding fast then slow. I moved side to side so that his dick could hit each curve my body possessed. He was taking my body somewhere it had never been. I turned around and started riding in reverse cowgirl. I was in pure ecstasy as I came for what seemed to be the fifth time. "Shit Dior, ride that dick." I felt his dick go soft, indicating that he had bust.

"Chance, why didn't you tell me to get up before you came?"

"Girl, I'm about to be your husband, ain't no pull out bih."

I got up and punched him in the arm, and he threw a pillow at me. I made a mental note to go grab a plan B pill in the morning. We already had three kids and didn't need anymore.

I went to hop in the shower so that I could get ready for bed. The kids were still tucked in tight so that was one less thing I had to worry about. He came and joined me and washed my back. I loved when his hands roamed my body and explored my curves.

"I love you so much Dior and I can't wait to say I do."

"Me neither babe. We have nine days left."

He kissed my forehead then he got out. "I have to go to the club for a while ma, but I will be back before you wake up."

"Okay, be careful babe and make sure you come home to us."

"Always." I washed my body down two more times before I got out. Dried off and put Shea Butter all over my body. I pulled my hair back into a ponytail since I had and appointment to get it done tomorrow. I couldn't wait to get my inches. I noticed I had a text notification from Chance.

Hubby: Goodnight my love. That pussy had a nigga about to cry tonight. (smiley face with tongue.)

Likewise, I love when we make love. Goodnight Mr. McCray

I laid down and pulled out my kindle. I had recently downloaded "Big and Aimee" and decided to read until I fell asleep. Big and Aimee reminded me so much of me and Chance. Sleep soon took over me and I fell asleep with my soon to be husband on my mind

King:

I couldn't believe the way my sisters were acting in public. I went into the basement to check my stash. I had a pretty fucked up day and needed a drink to help boost the highness that my body was about to endure. I went into my stash and scaled myself a 3.5 and locked it back up. I got my Dutch and split it open. I licked each end and rolled my blunt to perfection. I lit the blunt as I walked to my car and got in. I pulled off and headed to my club to chill for a while. I wasn't in a rush, so I consumed every inch of my blunt. About twenty minutes later, I pulled up to the club and parked out front. The line was long as hell, meaning that tonight would be a great night.

"CHANCE!" I scanned the crowd to see who was calling my name and saw that it was Diamond. Diamond was this stripper that I used to fuck with before my dealings with Dior started. We didn't end on bad terms or no shit like that, but she had to go.

"What's good ma?"

"Let me walk thru with you."

I chuckled at her suggestion. "Nah ma, you gotta wait like everybody else." I turned and walked inside. I didn't have a problem with the bitch, but what would that look like walking in with the next bitch when wifey was at home? I walked in and dapped up all my niggas and went to the bar.

"Yo Trice, let me get the Henny straight no chaser."

She gave me my drink and I walked towards my office. I spotted Cody over in VIP and he saluted me from the other side. I went to my office and sat down. As bad I hated it, the shit with Cali and Chasity took over my thoughts. I couldn't imagine how Cali felt finding out about her pops. My mother was wrong in every way, but the damage was done now. A knock graced my door.

"Come in."

Cody walked in and walked towards me. Considering that we still were on edge a little with one another, I put my hand on my piece.

"Let me holla at you, on a serious tip. And put that baby ass gun away, my nigga. If I wanted to hurt you, it would have been done." I didn't trust nobody, so I kept my hand where the fuck it was.

"I'm listening."

"Check this out. I don't know if my sister told you about my pops coming to the hospital when she was there, but I need you to check something out for me."

"Nah, I didn't know shit about that. The fuck was that nigga doing there?"

"That's what I'm trying to figure out. I know we ain't the best of friends and I'm not trying to be. My pops had a nigga with him and when she saw him, she freaked the fuck out. I need to know what was up with that. I know she not going to tell me because she brushes it off every time I ask but something not sitting right."

"I will try to get her to come thru with some info, but it's not guaranteed. You know how Dior can be."

"True shit." He dapped me up and turned to leave. Dior had some explaining to do. I finished up my paperwork and shot her a text.

We gotta talk.

Wifey: About?

I'm on my way.

I knew it was a family matter and it was probably none of my business, but for her to not tell me about her pops had me bothered. I pushed my Rarri to the limit on the e-way and got home in less than fifteen minutes. I jumped out of the car, barely cutting it off, and ran into the house.

"Damn, break the doorknob then. What the hell is wrong with you?"

"Nah, explain to me why you never mentioned your pops and some nigga coming to the hospital."

Her eyes instantly got glossy and my anger subsided. "I don't want to talk about it and would appreciate it if you and Dakota let the shit go."

"Fuck that. Who is the nigga?"

She went and took a seat on the couch and started explaining who the man was. Anger immediately took over as she told me how their pops traded her body to pay off his debts. "I'm going to kill that nigga."

"Chance, please calm down. Please, just let it go." I couldn't believe she would even ask me to spare the nigga that caused her so much pain.

"I'm not calming a motherfucking thing. Yo, get your brother on the line RIGHT FUCKING NOW."

"ALRIGHT CHANCE DAMN."

She called Cody and he answered on the first ring, "What up sis?"

"Nah, this King, pull up." I hung up before he could respond and I knew he would be here within thirty minutes. I sat down beside her as she laid her head on my chest and her tears soaked my shirt. No words were spoken as we waited for Cody to come over. I saw bright lights beaming outside of the window, so I got up to open the door. It was time to put all of our problems to the side because we had a serious conflict of interest.

"Come to the living room; you won't believe this shit."

He turned the corner then looked at me with hate in his eyes. "Why the fuck is my sister crying my nigga?"

"Chill the fuck out nigga. Don't create a problem in this bitch. She got something to tell your dumb ass."

He walked over and sat on the ottoman in front of his sister.

"Talk to me Dior."

"That man, that was at the hospital used to molest me. Daddy owed him money, so he used to let him feel on me and eat my pussy.

At the time, I didn't know what was going on because we were only nine years old. It continued until we turned eleven. Dakota, please just let it go; I don't want any more drama in my life." He was furious and his once light colored skin was the color of Satan. The veins were protruding from his neck and forehead.

"Let it go? I will let it go, alright. Come on sis, you know me well enough to know both of them niggas just as good as dead."

As much as I hated it, I was going to help dead this issue. "Aye, I'm riding too."

"Nah, I got it. You stay your ass right here."

"Nigga, she my responsibility as much as she is yours, so let's fucking go."

He stood there for a minute in deep thought. "Aight man fuck, come on but stay out of my way."

This nigga's mouth was literally going to be the death of him. She sat there not saying a word as I ran upstairs to get my AK-47. I was on a hunt for blood tonight.

Chapter 7

Bree:

I had completely lost myself and had a hard time finding Aubree. Dakota had texted and told me to dress nice and meet him downstairs in twenty. He had dropped the boys off with Dior for the weekend. I put on a black pair of Saint Laurent ripped jeans with a slim-fit button down. I put my hair up into a messy bun and did my make-up. I grabbed my Giuseppe Zanotti studded suede lace-up booties and my Giuseppe Zanotti tote, then headed downstairs.

"Damn baby, you look good as fuck."

"Thanks boo." He gave me a slight peck on my cheek and grabbed my hand. We got into the car and pulled off. I had no idea where we were going and I knew he wasn't going to tell me. After almost an hour of driving, we ended up at a field. There was a jet sitting there waiting.

"Dakota, what the hell is this? What are you up to now?"

"Stop asking all these damn questions woman and get on this damn jet."

"But, I don't have any clothes; you should have told me to pack."

"But, I got money and lots of it. You need a new wardrobe anyway. Look at what you have on girl; you looking like nobody loves you." He burst into laughter, yet I found nothing funny.

"Nigga, I look good. Fuck what you talking about." The jet took off into a destination unknown. I was missing my babies something terrible, but I guess he wanted some alone time. I would try to enjoy this little break as best that I could. After three hours, we arrived at the most beautiful place I had ever seen. The view was everything. We were in Punta Cuna.

"Dakota, it's beautiful. You remembered." On our first date, I told him that I always dreamed of coming here. Him remembering that meant so much to me.

"I told you I was going to make all of your dreams come true, Bree baby. Now, let's go to this room, so you can show me how thankful you are."

Cody:

After I left Dior's house the other night, my entire mental was fucked up. I couldn't believe the nigga I once looked up to allowed niggas to take advantage of his only daughter. I was skeptical about letting that nigga, King, ride with me, but I understood where he was coming from. We rode around in silence looking for Roberto's punk ass for hours until I finally gave up. I dropped King back off at the house and went straight home. I had something planned for my baby the next morning and couldn't wait to surprise her. We laid down and fell fast asleep. The next morning, we boarded the jet. She was so nervous because she didn't know what was in store for her. When we made it to our destination, the smile on her face made a nigga's heart smile because I was the reason.

"Dakota, it's beautiful. You remembered." On our first date, I told him that I always dreamed of coming here. Him remembering that meant so much to me.

"I told you I was going to make all of your dreams come true, Bree baby. Now, let's go to this room, so you can show me how thankful you are."

We made it to our room. She started kissing a nigga like she was hungry for the dick and I was going to be the nigga to feed her. She unzipped my pants and dropped to her knees. She stroked my lil nigga until he stood at full attention and took him into her mouth. If she couldn't do nothing else, she could suck a mean one. She was bobbing her head like one of them lil bobble head dolls. She had a nigga knees buckling and I fell back against the wall.

"Fuck." She was spitting on it and sucking the soul out of it. She bit down gently and started humming on my dick until she found the perfect rhythm. She went further down until all 9 inches were down her throat. "Shit girl." I shot a load down her throat and quickly picked her little ass up. I carried her to the sofa and threw her down. She quickly snatched off her pants and, of course, she ain't have on no panties. I slid in that fruit gusher and went to work. Stone cold fucking is what I was doing.

"Mm, Dakota." She was digging her nails in my back and biting my shoulder.

"Who got this pussy on lock?"

"Fuck, you do."

"Who the only nigga that can make that thang squirt?"

"You baby, I'm about to cum."

"Do that shit then. Paint it on baby." I started giving her them daddy love you long time strokes and sent her body into shock mode. Her legs started shaking like they were having a seizure. "Damn girl, this shit gets better every time." She started throwing it back and I started throwing it harder. She clamped her muscles down on my dick and we both stopped moving. I was about to start back until I felt her pussy give my dick a nut shower.

"Mm, shit." She leaned up and took my bottom lip into her mouth as I grinded slowly into her juice box. I felt my nut building and I started pumping fast. She started pushing at me, "Nah, hell nah Dakota get your ass up."

"Hold on, I'm almost done."

"No nigga because you not going to pull out."

I jumped up and she started smiling.

"Thank you."

"What you thanking me for? You full of cum baby."

I couldn't stand his ass.

Jas:

It had been almost a week since I had seen or heard from Carlos and I was pissed about it. He was acting like a little ass boy, getting mad at me for speaking facts. Hell, I was tired of him and my retarded ass baby daddy fake ass beef and putting me in the middle.

We were not in high school. He was the only one gave Dakota the satisfaction. I had just got off work and had an hour and a half before I picked Demi up from the daycare. I decided to go and get me a manicure and pedicure to waste time. I parked my car and got out. I was scrolling on Instagram and walking when I mistakenly bumped into somebody.

"Excuse me."

"Yeah I know. Watch where the fuck you going next time."

"Fuck that! I take my damn excuse back then hoe, since you being rude about it." She had a little sidekick with her, of course. Bitches loved to jump bad when they had an audience.

"Ooh sis, Los got him a feisty one this time. You might have some competition."

"Who the fuck is you?"

"Your worst nightmare bitch. Stay the hell away from my husband." She pushed me out of the way and started walking off until I yoked her ass up by her hair. I started pounding on her ass, throwing mean ass hooks. She fell and I started stomping her, then her little side chick pushed me off and I tumbled but caught myself from falling. I squared up to go toe to toe with her. She swung and missed. I grabbed her arm and swung her around so that her back was towards me. I started choking her from behind and the little bitch on the ground bit my leg. I let go of her friend and tried to attack again, but someone grabbed me. I was trying my hardest to break loose, but this person had a death grip on me.

Whoever the chick was ran up and karate kicked me in the stomach.

"You stay away from Carlos; you hear me? You home wrecking whore. I won't warn you again."

Did I hear her right? Carlos is married? We had been kicking it for about a year and for her to say she was his wife had me fucked up. "Get off of me." I walked to my car, forgetting about what I originally came for. I had about forty-five minutes, so I was headed to Los' dealership. He was about to give me some got damn answers. I was sick of these niggas and they hidden ass females. I hopped in my car, breaking every law that existed. My hair was disheveled, my shirt was ripped, and I had a scratch on my face. I was a grown ass woman and acting ratchet in public just wasn't going to cut it. I had a daughter that I had to set examples for. I pulled up to the lot and didn't even worry about cutting off my car; I just jumped out. He was with a customer but I didn't give a fuck.

"Excuse me, we need to talk, NOW!"

"Jasmine, what the fuck? I'm sorry sir; excuse me for a second." He grabbed my arm and pulled me towards his office.

"What the fuck happened to you?"

"Your wife is what fucking happened. How the fuck did you miss the detail that you had a whole wife around, Carlos? And a childish one at that. Why did that hoe try to come for me like I knew she existed? I should punch your ass in the face. Is that why your gator mouth ass been acting shady huh?"

"Hold up, calm the fuck down first off. Second, what do you mean my wife? I'm not fucking married; I'm separated. The bitch won't sign the papers." I started laughing to keep myself from swinging on this nigga.

"Separated? You never said shit about that so what you on?"

"Aye, I'm working right now so get at me later."

"Nah, I don't think I will. You can lose my number with your lying ass." I turned around and walked off. Once again, love had failed me. The man I had grown to love was legally taken and lied about it. I got in my car and headed to get my baby. I called my girl Dior because I seriously needed to vent.

"Hey baby mama, what's up?"

"Girl nothing. Are you at home? I need a vent session one on one?"

"Of course. Is everything ok boo?"

"Girl, hell no. I will tell you everything when I get there. I am so sick of these lying ass niggas."

"Aw hell, that type of vent session. Well, pull up bitch; let me grab the wine."

"Ok, let me pick up Demi and then I will be there." We hung up the phone as I pulled up to the daycare. This shit had me hot.

Los:

A nigga was so hot that I felt the steam coming out of my ears. I couldn't believe Jas came to my place of business with that bullshit. I was even more pissed that my stupid ass baby mama was in Atlanta and fucking up what I had going on. I was really tired of that stupid ass bitch. Me and Shawna had gotten married while I was in prison a couple years back, but the shit didn't last. When I came home, things with me and her wasn't the same and I tried to get a divorce, but she wasn't hearing that shit. She had fucked my cousin, Marco, on some revenge type of shit because she had found out that I had cheated on her. Marco ended up telling me about it and I ended the relationship right after. She did stupid shit, like try to keep my kids from me, and I took her to court for joint-custody. Her sister Bailay and their mother begged me to get full custody, but I didn't want to kick the shit that dirty. I had been trying to move on for years, but she would always run anybody I fucked with away. I couldn't let her do that shit with Jasmine. I loved Jas and wanted to be with her and that was what it was. I had been calling Shawna ever since Jas left, but she wouldn't answer. I called one last time and finally got an answer.

"Damn, you ain't been blowing up my line. I guess your little bitch told you how we beat her ass."

"Yo, why your dumb ass coming down here starting shit with my girl? You kicking it like a nigga still want you and you know that shit dead. You need to take your dumb ass back home."

"I am home nigga; I'm back for good."

"You out here wildin and shit. Where the fuck are my kids, dumb ass hoe?" I hated every piece of Shawna. As much as I loved my kids, I wish I hadn't gotten her pregnant.

"Ooh hubby, you must really like that black bitch huh? Fuck her, you know you miss me."

"I really don't." I was done talking to her dumb ass, so I hung up and sent her a text.

Sign the fucking papers.

Shawna: Nope. Till death do us part. (Kissy face)

I had to find a good lawyer that could get me out of this shit before she ruined my life. She was so unfit and childish. I never hated nobody as much as I hated her. I got in my car and headed to Jas' house. I knew I was the last person she wanted to see, but I didn't give a fuck. I wanted her to at least hear me out. I knew I was wrong for lying to her and not telling her I was married, but I had my reasons. It took me all of ten minutes to get there and it fucked me up because she wasn't there.

Chapter 8

Moe:

I had finally calmed my nerves and asked Dior to meet me at Chow Baby for lunch. She agreed and told me she would be there by noon. I had gotten an apartment in Mechanicsville, so I wasn't far from the restaurant at all. I hopped in the shower and washed with Dove soap. I had my extensions washed and colored yesterday and my inches were poppin. I got out of the tub and went into my closet to find something to wear. Shit, I need to take my ass shopping. I grabbed my PINK shorts set and flip flops and got dressed. After I was dressed, I looked myself over in the mirror and was satisfied. The only thing I hated was that the scar from where I was shot was still so visible. I grabbed my Fendi bag and headed out of the house. I sparked up a blunt and hopped on 75, headed to the restaurant. I pulled into a parking deck and paid for parking. I was walking towards the restaurant when a car damn near swerved onto the curb and hit me.

"Bitch." She stuck her middle finger up at me and jumped out of the car.

"I should have hit your ugly ass."

I started walking up to her when Dior grabbed my arm.

"India, is there a problem here?"

"It damn sure is. Dior, you know this triflin ass hoe?"

61

"Yes, I do. This is my sister, so like I said, is there a motherfucking problem?" Dior stepped in front of me and got into the mystery woman's face.

"So, you knew all about this hoe fucking my husband and didn't say shit? I know she had something to do with his murder; I just know she did."

"Who the fuck is your husband?"

Dior turned to face me. "Marco is her husband. India, let's be clear. I didn't know shit about her and, besides, let's not play like we the best of friends."

"Yeah hoe, MY husband and I know your home wrecking ass did something to him."

She swung and punched me in the jaw. All I saw was red and I started whooping her ass. I knew about her, but I never knew what she looked like. I didn't even know how she knew who I was.

Dior grabbed me and pushed the both of us back.

"Listen bitch, I look too damn good to be out here fighting and shit but swing at my sister again, and I am going to tag that ass. Try me India, you already know how I roll." I guess she did know because she backed her ass up.

"I saw her in his phone Dior; she was the last person he was with." The police pulled up and started asking questions. After taking a few of the witnesses' statements, they handcuffed India and took her away.

"I will find you. This is not your last time seeing me." I knew I would be seeing her again, but I didn't give a fuck. We walked off and walked into the restaurant. I knew we had unfinished business.

Dior:

I was a little pissed off with my brother for running his big ass mouth to Chance about Roberto coming to the hospital. I didn't want to make it seem like I was keeping secrets from my fiancé but, some things, I didn't want him to know. My past being one of them. I knew the both of them would flip out when they found out, but the damage was all done now. I was headed to meet up with Moe for lunch. We were actually getting better with our relationship and I was happy about that. The only thing that bothered me was that I knew she would soon want back the custody of Christian and I didn't think I was ready for that. I had grown so attached to him and looked at him as my own. I felt so sorry for him because this entire situation was beyond confusing. How ironic is it that his dad is also the father of his cousins/ siblings? This shit belonged on Jerry Springer.

When I pulled up to the restaurant, I saw Moe arguing with someone that looked familiar. I parked my car and jumped out, running full speed to where she was. I couldn't believe Marco's wife, India, had come for my sister. Moe was just about to run up when I grabbed her arm.

"India, is there a problem here?"

"It damn sure is. Dior, you know this triflin ass hoe?"

"Yes, I do. This is my sister, so like I said, is there a motherfucking problem?" Dior stepped in front of me and got into the mystery woman's face.

"So, you knew all about this hoe fucking my husband and didn't say shit? I know she had something to do with his murder; I just know she did."

"Who the fuck is your husband?"

Dior turned, facing me. "Marco is her husband."

Now, I knew that Moe was aware of his wife, but that didn't give this bitch the right to try to hit her with a car. India knew all about me, so she knew that I had no problem beating her ass if need be. They said what they had to say and India reached around me and punched Moe in her jaw. I ended up breaking them up before I ended up in jail for capital murder. I wasn't with that fighting shit anymore; I was too fine for that. I was shooting bitches now. The police came and took India into custody and we walked off into the restaurant. We seated ourselves and waited for our waiter.

"What the hell was that about, I wonder?"

"You heard that psycho. She thinks I had her husband killed. Hell, his ass deserved everything he got because he almost killed me. Enough about those sick bastard though, what's been going on?"

"Nothing much, just living life the best that I can. It's some crazy shit going on now and I am trying to stay clear from it."

"And what is that?"

"Dakota and Chance found out about our father doing some things to me when I was younger." I felt the tears building, but I tried my hardest to stop them.

"Wait, we have the same father too? This shit is crazy."

"No, I don't think so. When our mother told us about you, she didn't mention Roberto being your father, so I doubt it." She spit out her drink and grabbed her chest, as if she was having a heart attack.

"Roberto? Roberto is your father?"

"Don't tell me you know him?" The waiter came and took our drink orders as we waited for our cook to come do his thing.

"Is he mixed with anything?"

"Yess bitch. Oh my God, I can't believe that sick bastard is your father. He is evil, Dior, and I know that you are aware of that. There are some things about my past that I am ashamed of, but it made me who I am today. Since our mother left me, I went into the system. I went from foster home to foster home and was molested in each one. I finally got tired of it and ran away. I started prostituting my body to make ends meet and Roberto happened to be my number one client. I was only 15 and he was fucking me and paying me top dollar. He is sick Dior." I couldn't believe the shit I was hearing. This world was so small and I couldn't believe my sister was right under my nose. She was crying in the middle of the restaurant and my heart broke for her. I was going to make Roberto pay with his life for the pain he caused us.

"He got me pregnant numerous of times but would always take me to get an abortion. He used to whip my ass if I even thought about going against his demands. That man is a nightmare."

"I am so sorry Moe. He ruined my childhood too and I will never forgive him for it. I hate we didn't meet sooner. Everything is going to be ok now. We have found each other and I don't plan on going anywhere."

The cook finally arrived and we went into the restroom to get ourselves together.

"I can't believe we just had a damn therapy session in the middle of Benihana's. It has been a long ass day already." We both laughed and I gave her a hug. It actually felt good having an older sister. We ate and talked about everything under the sun. It felt awkward talking with her about Chance. We left the restaurant and proceeded to the nail shop. We spent the entire day getting pampered and even went and got matching tattoos. I was going to enjoy having her around. I could only hope that things remained good with us because I was trusting her with my heart.

Chapter 9

Cali:

Y'all don't know how far on the edge I am on seriously hurting Chasity. The disrespect from that little bitch was at an all-time high. It seemed like she wasn't tired of me beating her ass because she continuously wanted to try it. When I saw her and Nyrue back at that restaurant, it took the angel on my shoulder to keep me from shooting the both of their asses. Then, the little broad that was with them wanted these hands to bless her body too. I was over the both of them and there was nothing nobody could do or say to make me change my mind. I was still on papers and was not about to continue to risk my freedom behind that thot and that no good ass nigga. I'm too fine for all of that. Joyce kept questioning me about the entire situation, but I didn't feel like talking about it anymore.

I heard music thumping loud outside, so I got up and went to the window. Unfortunately, it was Chance and I knew he was about to start his bullshit. I was happy that Chasity was gone because I knew he was going to try to play like he was a damn therapist and it was not safe for me to be around her ass right now. I heard him coming up the stairs. I laid down on the bed quickly and tried to play sleep. He burst into my room without knocking and snatched the covers off of me.

"Get yo dumb ass up. You know damn well you not sleep. Don't play with me, Cali. I saw your childish ass in the window, now what the fuck is you and Chasity's problem?"

"Fuck Chasity. Your little sister ain't nothing but a hoe."

"Is that right? So, you just gone let a nigga come between you and your blood? Where the fuck they do that at?"

"It's more to it than that. She tried to come onto him in my fucking face so no, I am not fucking with her. She is dead to me."

"Yo, you sound dumb as fuck. Fuck that nigga, Cali. Niggas come a dime a dozen but family here to stay. And what's up with you and ma?"

"Fuck her too. How could she lie about who my dad was for all these damn years? That's foul bro and you know it. I can't trust no damn body and I'm tired of being surrounded by snakes. Nobody gave a fuck about me when I was in jail, then I find out my sister been trying to fuck my dude and my mother is a liar. Fuck this whole family." I was beyond emotional at that moment and the tears started to overflow. Chasity had really fucked me up with this one. I went under my mattress and got a blunt so that I could roll up.

"So, you smoke now Cali? Come on sis, this shit ain't you. You too pretty to be stressing over a nigga."

I wasn't listening to nothing he was saying and that was that. There was no love nor hope left for this family.

"Get up and get dressed. You coming to my house for a few days until you cool off. You can hang out with Dior and Moe."

"What the fuck? Why are they even hanging with each other?" I was confused as hell because the last I remember, those two hated each other.

"You wouldn't believe it if I told you, but they real sisters."

"Real sisters? Moe adopted right?"

"Yeah, she was adopted but they have the same mother. I know that shit still haven't set in with me either."

"Oh hell nah. What's up with you and Rue fucking sisters?"

"Don't compare me to that nigga sis, real shit." All I could do was shake my head because that was some crazy shit.

"Y'all need to go on Jerry." I laughed at my damn self. I got up and went into my closet to get my shoes. We walked down the stairs and headed outside. *This bitch.* Chasity was getting out of the car and I sat there minding my lil business.

"Where you about to go?"

"To the house. You want to ride?"

"No, she don't," I answered before she even had the opportunity. I didn't want her near me for the moment.

"Cali, can we talk?"

"No, we cannot. I don't understand why all of a sudden everybody wanted to talk. Her, out of all people, had no reason to even think that we could reconcile.

"Chasity, you don't know how much you hurt me. I knew it was something that you were so interested in. I will always love you but, right now, I am not ready to talk about it." My brother made me let her in the car and we pulled off. We pulled up to this bad ass mini mansion.

"And you say your ass don't have no check. Big bro got good cash, let me hold some nigga."

"Shut up and get out of the car." We all got out and walked towards the door. Dior met him at the door with my nephew Carson and I instantly grabbed him and walked off.

"What up bae?" Dior was looking confused and Chasity was standing at the door with her arms folded with an attitude.

Chance looked at her and shook his head. "Aye Chas, chill with that extra shit." I had completely forgotten about Chas not liking Dior. She didn't even know why she didn't like her, but I guess it was because she was Team Moe. Come to think about it; they are just alike, so maybe that was why they were so tight. I went and sat on the couch with Carson in my arms. Cayleigh and Christian were sitting on the floor watching TV. I couldn't believe my brother had all these damn kids. Everybody came and sat down when the doorbell rang. I knew, right then, that Moe had arrived.

Jas:

It had been a few weeks since I had talked to Carlos and I was beyond pissed about it. The first couple of days he had been hitting my line non-stop, but I wasn't ready to talk to his ass. Now that I was ready to hear him out, he was not answering my calls. I hadn't heard from Dior in a while and we had so much to catch up on. Dakota was on his way over to drop Demi off and I was happy about that. I had missed my little diva something terrible this weekend. I was at the island watching TV when my doorbell rang. I was only expecting Dakota, so I didn't bother looking through the peephole. I opened the door and stepped to the side so that he could come in. I tried my hardest not to pay attention to the fact that he was looking sexy as fuck right at that moment. Demi was sleeping in her seat, and I grabbed her and laid her in her swing.

"What it do Jas? You good?"

"Yep, did y'all enjoy the weekend?"

"Always. Baby girl be thugging it when she be with her big brothers and daddy. I bought her some more milk; it's in the bag."

"Ok thanks. You look nice today." He stood back and started staring at me with his hand under his chin, as if in thought."

"So do you, but you look different."

"Different?"

"Hell yeah. You glowing or some shit. That nigga ain't got you pregnant, huh?"

"Hell no. No skinny dipping this way. I am not ready for another baby just yet." I didn't tell him about me and Los splitting because it wasn't his business. I was still conflicting with myself on whether or not I even wanted to further what we had. I didn't know what Dakota had on me, but I seemed to always gravitate to him. He

71

was my weakness. I sat there staring him in his eyes, like we were having a stare off. He leaned in and kissed me on my lips. We kissed so passionately, like we missed each other for all of five minutes. He snatched back, but it didn't take away the fact that my cat was leaking something serious.

"Shit, I can't do this shit with you, Jas. I'm engaged to be married and I'm sitting here fucking up. Let me take my ass home."

"You right, I apologize." He walked to the door and left out. I went back and sat on the sofa, thinking about what had just happened. Here I was building a relationship with Bree and, the next minute, I'm kissing her fiancé. A part of me felt bad as fuck. I grabbed my phone to scroll social media when my doorbell rang again. *Now who the hell could this be?* I looked through the peephole and Dakota had come back. I opened the door for him.

"Did you leave…" He grabbed both sides of my face and stuck his tongue down my throat. He started stripping me out of my clothes as I did the same to him. He fell back on the stairs and I straddled him. He grabbed a condom and slid it down his shaft and I hopped aboard. My pussy immediately clamped down and creamed his dick. His eyes rolled to the back of his head.

"Fuck." I started grinding nice and slow, careful to feel every inch of the dick that I sincerely missed.

"Mm, I missed this so much."

"Me too. Nah, for real, this going to always be mine."

I picked up the speed; I felt my body shaking. "I'm about to cum again."

"Do that shit then. I wanna feel all of it." I let out all that I had as he flipped me over and went back in with no warning. He was beating my guts and I felt every bit in my stomach.

"Yess, right there."

"Put that ass up higher." I arched my back some more and felt his dick poking my soul.

"Shit girl. You squeezing the fuck out of my dick." He gave five more pumps and I felt his kids shoot inside the condom. We both sat on the steps all out of breath.

"Damn girl. You got a nigga cheating and shit."

"You brought your horny ass back over here, so don't blame your ain't shit ways on me." We started laughing and woke Demi up. I threw on my t-shirt while he went upstairs to wash off. He came back downstairs and kissed us both goodbye. As soon as he left, my phone notified me that I had a text message.

Baby daddy: *Can you please keep that between us? And keep that thang tight for me. (tongue out emoji)*

Shut up. Bye Dakota

I fed Demi and she fell back asleep. I went and hopped in the shower and let the hot water hit my body. I stayed in the shower for over thirty minutes, until my skin wrinkled. I got out and put cocoa butter all over my body. My phone started ringing, but it was a private number. I quickly hit ignore because I didn't answer those. I started walking off and the unknown caller called right back.

"Who is this?"

"You fuck that nigga like you fuck me? You ain't nothing but a hoe."

"Excuse me? You have some nerve to call my phone talking that bullshit when you got a whole wife. Shouldn't you be on her line with the bullshit?"

"I should have known you wasn't shit. You played with the wrong nigga." He hung up before I could respond. Now, I had to worry about him running his big mouth since he saw us.

Chapter 10

Cody:

Damn, I slipped up and gave Jas the dick and I knew shit was bound to go left. She couldn't hold fucking water, so I knew it would come out sooner or later. A nigga was just tired of fighting the temptation when it came to her. When I left her house, I drove around, trying to convince myself that I was over her. I couldn't do it, so I went to the store and got a rubber. I wouldn't dare skinny dip because I had super sperm, and Lord knows I wasn't trying to get her pregnant. Having sex with her made old feelings resurface and now I was all fucked up. I had so much shit on my mind, from my love life to the situation with my sister, that a nigga was stressing heavy. Dior had sent a text telling me to stop by, so I was on my way to her house. I stopped by the liquor store and got a 6-pack of Natural Ice. I was trying to keep her happy by remaining cordial with King. I pulled up to her house and there was an extra car in the driveway. I knocked on the door and a bad bright red bitch with red hair opened the door. She had grayish looking eyes. Shawty was sexy as a muhfucka.

"You coming in or are you just going to stand there and stare at me?" I snapped out of my trance when I realized she was trying to turn up.

"What the fuck? Aye, lil girl, I didn't sleep with your funky ass, so don't kick that attitude shit with me. Move out my got damn way with your bald head rude ass." I nudged her out of my way. She was too bad to have the fucked up attitude she had.

"Hey, how you doing? You must be Dior's twin brother?"

"What you think? Who the hell are y'all anyway?"

"Hold the fuck up now. I didn't do shit to you."

"My bad ma, you right. It's Strawberry Shortcake with no edges right there just pissed me off. Who you?"

"I'm Cali and that's Chasity. We are Chance's sisters."

"Cool. Where my sister at anyway?"

"They upstairs."

King's baby mama, Moe, came down the stairs and looked my way.

"Hey Cody."

"What up."

I stood against the wall and waited for Dior to come down. I was trying to figure out why the hell all of these people was over her like it was a family reunion or some shit. They finally came down the stairs and Dior walked my way.

"I haven't seen you in forever nigga. You acting funny, what's up?"

"Y'all having family therapy or some shit. What's going on?"

"Nah, it's a lot going on. But I did invite you over, so you could get to know Moe more."

"I know her. She my sister and she your baby daddy baby mama, so what else is there to know?" She punched me in the arm.

"Dakota, chill the fuck out. She is just as much your sister as I am, so don't do her like that."

"Yeah aight."

Moe walked over and stood next to Dior. "Is it a problem? I didn't do shit to you, so you can stop being salty with me. I am just as lost as you are."

"Aye ma, stay out of this, aight. Nah, ain't no problem, everything quite kosher on my end." We sat with each other at the dining table and caught up on a couple of things. She told us the bullshit about Roberto and I was itching even more to kill his pussy ass. I didn't see how his perverted ass managed to live a whole different life outside of his family. His time was coming and it was coming soon.

"Aight y'all, let me get my ass home before wifey start calling. I will catch up to y'all later." I left out and got in my car. I was sitting there rolling a blunt when the chick Chasity knocked on my window.

"What your lil high yellow ass want?"

"Chill out nigga. I came to apologize, but don't make me take the shit back."

"Take it back then, baby girl; a nigga not gone cry."

"You are such an asshole."

I rolled my window back up and pulled off. King needed to check his sister with her fast ass. I had enough sense to know she wanted this good shit. I was too sexy for her not to. I lit my blunt as I hit the highway blasting Do or Die "Do U".

23's like Jordan on the Escalade

Got a pound of dro' girl, if you wanna blaze

You can let your hair down, while the AC blow

Before you get in, I just need to know

Do you? (Do you? Do you? Do you?)

I'll keep it on the low

Do you? Do you

I made it to the house and went inside. "Bree, baby, where you at?"

"In the laundry room, hold up." She came into the kitchen and leaned up to give me a kiss.

"Where the twins?"

"Sleep, thank God. They are bad as hell, thanks to you."

"Yeah whatever. Why you didn't cook?"

"Don't come in here trying to check shit when you didn't even look in the oven."

I opened the oven and it was her good ass homemade lasagna. I was high as fuck and had the munchies, so I was about to go nothing but in. I went to wash up while she fixed my plate. I went upstairs to change my pants and put on a wife beater. I changed my clothes and went to take a piss. I came out of the bathroom and Bree was standing there with tears in her eyes.

"Why Dakota?" She pulled out the condom wrapper that I had from Jas' house.

"Shit."

Los:

Jasmine had a nigga more than fucked up if she thought that I was going to let her get away with this shit. She been mad with a nigga about some shit that she didn't even have facts on. Shawna knew damn well we had been separated for years, so to cause drama between me and what I thought was my lady was fucked up. I needed space, so I had been avoiding Jas. I was going to her house to talk shit out with her and explain everything. When I saw her and that lame ass nigga fucking on the steps, I was livid. I thought I had a loyal bitch, but she was far from it. She couldn't wait for us to split to open her legs for his lame ass, even though she tried to convince me she was over him. I should have known she was lying though because she was so weak for that nigga. I took a couple of weeks off work so that I could handle shit with my lawyer and try to get this divorce settled. I was going to pay Shawna to sign those papers. She was the type that would literally do anything for a dollar. I was going by her sister's house to discuss a number that she would accept to sign them so that I could move on with my life. Bailey had told me that Shawna wanted to take my kids away for good, so it was a matter of time before I took her ass to court. She wanted to play games, then I was all for it. I was filing for full custody.

I pulled in and she was outside with two niggas. *How the fuck did I end up with this thot?* Every time I turned around, she was with a different nigga and that was far from safe for my kids.

"Shawna, where my kids at?"

"In the house. Hey to you too. That's my crazy ass baby daddy. I will see y'all later. Call me." The dudes got in the car and pulled off.

"Why you always got all these niggas around the kids? That shit ain't safe stupid ass girl."

"Whatever, you just jealous. What did you come here for?"

"Jealous of what? Girl, I don't want you. I only care about my kids' safety. Remember that. You always been a little thot; I just thought I could change you but I couldn't. I came to talk about these papers."

"What about them? Don't tell me you came all the way over here hoping I would sign them. I lost those damn papers Carlos."

"You didn't lose shit. Why won't you sign them? It's not like I'm going to change my mind about it; I really don't want you."

"That's what you say now. Why you want me to sign them so bad? You trying to marry that home wrecker?"

"Home wrecker? There wasn't a home for her to wreck slow ass girl. Fuck that! Look, how much you want to sign them?"

"I don't want no damn money. I want our family."

This shit was a lose lose situation and I was over it. She was about to make me go back to that old nigga I tried so hard to leave behind. I walked in the house and spent time with my kids before I left. These bitches were going to be the death of me.

Rue:

Cali had called and asked if I could come get her from her brother's spot. I didn't know what that was about, but I grabbed my .9 and hopped in the car. I plugged the address into my GPS and headed there. I hoped that, when I got there, it wasn't any bullshit and we could talk like two adults. I missed my baby and wanted shit to get back to normal. This wasn't like us to be fighting all the damn time. Cali was my world. Thirty minutes later, I pulled up to a mini mansion. *This bitch lit.* King's house was shitting on any house I had ever had. I text and told her that I was outside and waited for her to come out. She finally came out and got in the car, looking upset.

"You good?"

"Yes, just get me home please."

"Can we please talk ma?"

"Talk." I put the car in reverse and pulled out of the driveway.

"Listen Calz, I am so sorry for everything. I apologize for not telling you about your sister, but I didn't want y'all to be like y'all are now. I knew how much love you had for your sister and I would never jeopardize that. You mean the world to me baby and I am so sorry for hurting you. As far as the jail issue goes, I hate I made you feel like I didn't care. I would never turn my back on you and you know that. When you told me not to come down there, I got caught up in the money and forgot what was important. I miss you so much baby. I miss waking up hearing your voice and that beautiful smile. I love you, Calz; you gotta know a nigga sorry." She was crying and I reached over and wiped her eyes.

"I am just so tired of everybody betraying me. You really hurt me Nyrue."

"I know baby and I'm sorry." I pulled into her driveway and we sat and talked a little more. "You want to come home with me?"

She shook her head yes and I pulled back out the driveway. She had plenty of clothes at my crib, so she didn't need them. We made it to the house and we fucked all night long. I had my girl back and she wasn't going nowhere ever again.

Chapter 11

Dior:

Moe had been spending a lot of time at our house since we were building a relationship. I felt kind of crazy trusting her around Chance, due to their history, but I highly doubted that either of them would play Russian Roulette with their lives and try me. I was pissed that Dakota had showed his ass the way he did by treating her like all of this was her fault. I was sure going to confront him about it. I had scheduled a girl's day out with all the girls and couldn't wait to hang. Bree and Jas were going to meet up with me and Moe at the spa. I was well overdue for some tender hands to rub down my body, since my man was always so busy. We also had to go to the venue to make sure everything fell through. My wedding was in less than five days and I was ecstatic. I got dressed, throwing on a mini sundress and my MK sandals. My hair was wild and curly. Of course, I filled in my brows and put on some MAC boyfriend stealer lipstick. I grabbed my Birkin bag and went downstairs to wait for Moe. After twenty minutes, she finally came downstairs and she looked stunning. She had on a denim Bodycon dress with a pair of Xena denim gladiator sandals. Her inches were in wand curls and her make-up was flawless.

"Your face is beat by the Gods. You going to have to hook me up Saturday."

"Thanks sis. Sorry it took so long; are you ready?"

"Yeah, let's ride. The nanny took the kids to the park."

We got in the car and headed to the spa. This was about to be an interesting day. We made it to the spa, and Jas and Bree were sitting in their cars. They got out when we walked up. Jas looked at Moe with a confused look and I knew she was trying to figure out who Moe was.

"Hey y'all. This is my older sister, Moe. Moe, this is Dakota's fiancée Bree, and his daughter's mother Jasmine." Everybody said their hellos as we walked inside the spa. We were instructed to undress and lay on the beds that were assigned. We had hour sessions, so we laid down and relaxed and let the masseuse take control.

"My best friend has been distant. What's up with that?"

"Don't start Jas," I said with a smile. "I have just been spending a lot of lost time with Monique. Don't take it personal."

"Understood. So, y'all got tested?" I had never even thought about that until at that moment when Bree mentioned it. I guess I didn't want to have that on my conscience if it came out that she wasn't my sister. I had gotten so used to being around her.

"No, we never thought about that."

"Well, you should before y'all get too close."

"Ok, what the fuck is this? Can y'all chill? If we wanted that, we would have done all of that. Are y'all mad or something?" Moe was pissed and I understood completely. You would think she would have been happy that I found my sister, but she seemed a bit salty.

"Alright damn, I was just trying to help you out."

"Well, it's not needed. Can we change the subject and enjoy ourselves please?"

"Are you ready for Saturday?" I smiled at the thought that, in a couple of days, I would be Mrs. Chance McCray.

Bree cleared her throat. "Speaking of Saturday, I don't know if I can make it."

I snapped my head in her direction because I knew that this bitch didn't say what I thought. "Excuse me? You what?"

"I said I can't make it. Something came up last minute that I have to take care of."

"Let me get this straight. You wait until the week of my wedding to tell me that you won't be in attendance? Oh, you got me fucked all the way up. Does Dakota know about this?"

"Calm down Dior. I don't have to tell him every move I make so, no, he doesn't know. I'm sorry, but this is important."

I had steam coming from my ears; I was livid. She had been acting weird lately but to tell me some bullshit like this threw up red flags with her.

"Oh yeah Jasmine, did you sleep good last night?" She smirked at Jas and turned her head. Bree was seriously on some more shit, coming for everybody when this was supposed to be a girl's day.

"What the fuck is that supposed to mean?"

"Why so upset? It's not like I fucked your man."

"Jas, what is she talking about?" Jasmine better not had slept with Dakota again but the look on her face was quite evident that she had indeed.

"I don't know what you're talking about, so don't come for me."

"Bitch, you know damn well you fucked my fiancé yesterday when he dropped Demi off. Here I was, trying to be an adult about all this and you sneaking your little thot ass behind my back, fucking my man. The part that pisses me off the most is that you could sit here and smile in my face, like you were not just bouncing on what belongs to me not even 24 hours ago. Once a hoe, always a hoe."

"You know what, fuck this shit." Jasmine stood up and started putting her clothes on. This had been the worst day of my life.

"Neither one of us is pregnant anymore, so we can fight it out if you want to, Aubree. You don't scare shit over this way."

Bree jumped up and wrapped the towel around her. Jas turned to walk off but was snatched back by Bree. They started going blow for blow and Bree's ass and titties were everywhere. They were straight whooping each other's ass. Straight box action, no hair pulling. We finally broke it up and Jas spit in Bree's face. She snatched away and started round two.

Bree:

It wasn't my intentions to go start some shit at the spa, but I just couldn't take Jasmine smiling in my face being fake. That irked my soul like hell. I had already put Dakota's ass out of my house and called off the engagement. I was no longer about to play games with his cheating ass. If he wanted her ugly ass so bad, he was now free to be with her. All the begging on bended knees he did fell on deaf ears. I didn't want to hear that shit because it was crystal clear that he wouldn't change. I didn't mean to let my anger take over and swing on the bitch but fakeness deserved to be handled. We were fighting like two niggas on the street, and Dior and Moe pulled us off of one another. I had calmed myself down until she had the audacity to spit on me. I lost it and charged at her again. She fell, and I jumped on top of her and started ramming her head into the floor.

"Nasty ass hoe." The women that were giving us our massages were screaming for help and Dior grabbed me. While she was pulling me off of Jas, I kicked her and she grabbed my leg and bit me. I screamed in agony because she had literally locked her mouth on my leg and sunk her teeth in. I wanted to literally kill her ass when I saw my leg bleeding.

"I will fucking kill you, Jasmine. You ain't never gone be shit but a side hoe. You can fuck and suck him dry and he still won't choose you."

"Bitch please. You don't know shit. Let me go Dior; I'm out of here." She walked out and Dior walked out behind her. Moe was just standing there shaking her head.

"Are you going to be ok? Trust me, I know how you feel."

"No, I won't be ok. I hate the both of them. I don't want anything to do with none of you motherfuckers." I stormed out, not giving a damn that I had just taken my anger out on the wrong person. It was all good though because revenge was coming and it was coming hard.

Moe:

That whole situation just caught me all off guard. The entire girl's day out was cut short because they didn't know how to act. The way they just put hands on each other had my ass shocked. Those were some crazy ass women. Bree slick pissed me off, going off on me like I fucked Cody and I didn't appreciate that shit one bit. I had my own issues going on, so I wasn't about to stress their problems. I had to figure out a way to get close to Cody as I had gotten with Dior. I really enjoyed every moment spent with my sister. Even though we were getting close, I felt bad because I had been keeping quiet about catching up with Roberto. I didn't say anything because I wanted to take care of him by myself. I was probably playing a dangerous game, but I didn't give a fuck. I knew he had a house out in McDonough, so I was putting a plan in motion. He played a major role in the way I turned out and I wasn't happy with myself. Telling Dior my biggest secrets made me feel a little better, but I still felt insecure with myself. I was just tired of feeling defeated with my life.

Chapter 12

King:

Thinkin' about them licks I hit, I had to

Thinkin' about if you was here, I had you, savage

Gon' roll it up my nigga

Roll up, jump out the car, squeeze the trigger

Gon' roll it up my nigga

Roll up, hop out the car, squeeze the trigger

I can hear the purple callin'

I was sitting in my office listening to Future's "Perky's Calling" playing on the loud speakers. I stood up and walked over to the window that overlooked the entire club. Business was doing numbers and I was getting richer. I was getting married in less than 48 hours and a nigga was getting cold feet. Me and Dior had come so far from where we started. There was no doubt in my mind that I wanted her to be my wife. The only thing that bothered me more than anything was the fact that we had yet to locate her perverted ass daddy. I was beyond ready to plant a couple of hot ones in that nigga. I heard a knock on the door and told them to come in.

"Moe? What you doing here? Is Christian ok?"

"Yeah, he is fine. I came to talk to you about something important." Ever since she had been back around, we had not talked much.

"Oh aight, so what is there to talk about then?"

"We can be friends Chance. No need to be rude. But anyway, did Dior say anything else about Roberto?"

"Nah, why you asking about him?"

"Please don't say anything, but I know where one of his houses are."

"Swear? Take me to him right fucking now." I immediately got angry. I would love nothing more than to tell my wife on our wedding day that all of her problems were gone.

"Wait a second, calm down. I had been staking out over there and he hasn't been there in two days. I know for a fact that he stays there though. I wanted to do it alone, but I got nervous. We can go if you want, but you have to promise to let me handle him. This is me and Dior's problem, not yours."

"There is no Dior without me, Moe; what the fuck you mean? We are one, so her problems are my problems." I put all of the papers in the safe and cleaned off my desk. I was ready to go handle that nigga at this moment and would not sleep until his blood was on my hands. We walked out of the office as Dior walked in. She stood there with anger evident on her face.

"Somebody mind telling me what's going on here?"

She shifted her weight over to one leg and folded her arms over her chest. I didn't have time to waste, so I grabbed her hand. "Let's go, I will explain in the car."

"No Chance. I said just me and you. I don't want Dior in any of this. Please Dior, just let us take care of this."

"Take care of what? Look Moe, I hope you don't take offense and if you do, oh well. I know you my sister and all, but I don't trust NOBODY alone with my man. At the end of the day, you are still his baby mama and you might miss the dick. Take it how you want but either I go or he doesn't, your choice."

Moe smacked her teeth and walked off in front of us. "Come on then."

We got into the car and I ran everything down to Dior. She wasted no time taking her gun out of her purse and making sure it was loaded.

"Yo, what the fuck Dior? Why do you have that?" "What you mean?"

"I thought we discussed that you were not carrying that shit around. You want to be Cleo so fucking bad."

"Chance, I don't want to hear that right now. I have to protect myself. You act like I'm walking around just shooting at muhfuckas or something. I am a woman and niggas like to take advantage of us, so I need protection."

"Get a fucking taser gun and pepper spray like a normal female then."

"Whatever. I am a grown ass woman and I am keeping Brittany, whether you like it or not. You kill me trying to run some shit; you better leave me alone."

We pulled up in McDonough and sat outside of the house Roberto was supposed to be staying at.

"Moe, you sure that nigga stay here? This shit looks abandoned."

"Yes Chance, damn."

We sat there for twenty minutes, then I saw a light come on and jumped out of the car. I was ready to get this shit over and done with. Dior and Moe got out and came running behind me. I wasn't with all that picking locks and climbing through windows, so I did shit the old fashion way and rang the doorbell. It took about ten minutes for him to open the door. He opened the door and I pushed him back inside with my gun in his face. He had his hand up as Dior and Moe walked in.

"Monique? What the fuck is this?"

"Shut the fuck up. Don't say shit to her."

Dior walked up to him and spit on him. "You little bitch. You an ungrateful ass bitch. After all of the shit I did for you, you bring these motherfuckers here to kill me?"

"And you a pervert. You were fucking my sister when she was just a child nasty ass bastard. What did you do for me? Let your wrinkled dick ass friends molest me for their own pleasure?"

93

"Sister?" He smirked then burst into laughter. "That whore is not your sister. Believe that shit if you want to, Dior. You didn't have no damn sister."

"My mother told me all about it, so stop fucking lying to me."

"Your sister died at birth. Your mother was so hell bent that Monique was her daughter but trust me, she is not. She is actually your cousin. I have a sister that was pregnant at the same time that your mother was. They were very close, the best of friends. They went in labor the same day, but your sister didn't make it. Shan tried to convince me to take Monique from your aunt, but I just couldn't do it. Your aunt felt so bad about your sister's death that she gave Moe up for adoption. If you don't believe me, go find her. Her name is Carole Baker. I am sorry you never knew about her, but this bitch is not your sister."

"So, you had sex with your own niece? You are one sick ass man. You are about to pay for all the pain you put me through."

"Fuck the both of you. Neither of you meant shit to me anyway. You came to kill me when the motherfucker that killed your mother is still walking."

"Who killed my mother?" Dior walked closer to him and placed her gun against his head.

"His name is Moto. He hires contract killers. He killed your mother because she went against him. She wouldn't kill Dakota. You will never find him because he moves around too much. He never stays still, but I know that he did it." She stepped back and lifted her gun, then gave Roberto 2 shots the head. She fell to her knees in tears and my heart broke for her. Moe stood there shaking and I pulled her into my arms. I didn't expect for that nigga to say the type of shit that he said. He deserved to burn in hell for the pain he caused them. Even though I loved Dior, my heart broke for Moe even more because she was back at square one. To be sleeping with your own uncle and be oblivious to it was disgusting.

"Come on y'all, we have to get out of here." I let go of Moe and pulled Dior off the floor. Moe was just standing there like she was lost. I understood her pain, but this wasn't the place to be stuck.

"MOE, LET'S GO."

She snapped out of it and came running. We all jumped in the car and I peeled out. Now, all I had to figure out was where the fuck the other nigga was. Nobody that caused harm to my baby was safe and I would not sleep until I had that nigga's head on a platter. We pulled up to the house and Cody was sitting in the driveway smoking a blunt. Dior got out and ran over to his car.

"Yo, what the fuck is wrong with my sister?"

Cody:

I had been staying back at my condo for the past two weeks since Bree put my ass out. She straight went loco on my ass about that condom wrapper before she even let me explain. She burned majority of a nigga's clothes and sliced up my shoes with a razor. I knew her ass was crazy but, damn, she went in. I was all types of bitch niggas that night. Jasmine had called and told me all about the fight that they had been in and I wasn't surprised. I knew Bree was going to pop off when she saw her. I understood her not wanting to be with a nigga after all that I put her through, but the fact that she was keeping my kids from me was fucked up. She wouldn't even let me talk to my boys and that shit had me going crazy.

I got up and got dressed and headed over to my sister's spot before I went to the club. That was another crazy ass situation because she had Moe all up in her shit and she didn't even know her. I understood that they wanted to bond and shit, but did she have to stay there? I didn't understand women and their way of thinking. I pulled in at Dior's crib and neither of the cars were in the driveway. I knew she would be home sooner or later, so I let my seat back and sparked up a blunt. I took that entire joint to the head and started vibing to the music that played in my head. After sitting there thirty minutes, I sparked up another blunt and started scrolling through my phone. I was so busy playing with the phone that I didn't see Dior walking towards my car until she was damn near at the window. I noticed that she looked bothered and had been crying. I jumped out of the car in defense mode.

"Yo, what the fuck wrong with my sister?"

"Calm down Cody. We got him."

Dior had specks of blood all over her and I started panicking.

"What the fuck? Got who? Aye, what the fuck is going on?"

King and Moe just stood there looking stupid and it pissed me off more. I pulled my gun off my waist and pointed it at the both of them.

"What is wrong with my sister and why does she have blood all over her clothes?"

"My nigga, you better put that shit down if you don't plan on using it. You got five seconds to get that gun out of my got damn face or it's about to be a major problem."

"Yeah, whatever nigga, start talking."

Dior grabbed my other arm and pulled me in the other direction. She started telling me about what had just happened and what Roberto said before she killed him. That shit had me fucked up, yet mad at the same time.

"Why did you take your ass out there Dior? I told you I had it."

"It was spur of the moment Cody. Please understand that I did what I had to do."

As much as I wanted to understand where she was coming from, I just couldn't. I wanted to be the one to pull the trigger and take that nigga out.

"I knew she wasn't a sister of mines. I knew the truth would come out sooner or later."

"Aww shut up, you didn't know shit. You think you know every got damn thing but you don't. I am happy I am not your sister neither, bitch nigga."

"This bitch nigga slaps bitches so tread lightly."

I still didn't too much care for Moe because at the end of the day, she was the cause of my nigga Drake being gone. Nobody would ever understand how much that shit still affected me on a daily basis. The trust for these niggas out here didn't exist since he was my right hand. She still was suspect in my eyes, family or not. Dior was naïve when it came to other people and that was a problem with me. He was her fiancé's baby mama for Christ's sake, so how could she trust her?

"I will be the last bitch you ever slap."

"Yeah whatever. You alright though, sis? I'm sorry you been through so much, but you need to be more careful making these type of decisions." I would never steer my sister in the wrong direction and that was the difference between me and King. He acted before he thought. There was no way he should have taken her to kill that nigga without knowing what they were getting into.

"Yeah, I'm good. I'm just happy it's all over and I can move on with my life."

"True. Aye, take a ride with me right quick though. I need to rap with you about some shit." I know I had told Jas not to run her mouth, but I needed her advice more than ever. A part of me wanted to fix shit with Bree, while the other part wanted to let it go.

"Umm, Moe, you can leave until I get back."

"Leave?"

"Yes, leave. You can't think that you are staying here with Chance alone."

"Nobody wants Chance, Dior. I am over all of that."

"That may be very much true, but it doesn't change the fact that you still need to leave." Moe smacked her teeth and crossed her arms. King smirked and shrugged his shoulders.

"Fuck it, I need to head to the club anyway." He got in his car and pulled off, and I did the same.

"So, what do you need to talk about?"

"I fucked up sis. I need advice."

Chapter 13

Dior:

I had been pissed off since Bree and Jasmine ruined my spa day because they wanted to be childish. I was so tired of them to the point that I didn't want neither of them around me anymore. It hurt me that they couldn't put whatever differences they had to the side, if only for one moment so that I could enjoy myself. I guess I was just lost as to what the problem was in the first place. I thought that we had overcome all of the drama, but I guess that shit was all a front. All I knew was that I didn't have anything to say to either of them until further notice.

I was at home with the kids when I decided to surprise Chance at the club. I called the nanny over and got dressed. I threw on a pair of ripped jeans and a denim button down. She finally made it over as I was walking down the stairs. "Good evening Samantha, the kids are bathed and sleeping."

"Thank you Ms. Dior."

I grabbed a pair of Giuseppe heels, my purse, and headed out. I pulled up to the club and stepped out.

"Hey Mrs. McCray, come on in."

I walked inside the club and headed towards Chance's office as he and Moe walked towards me.

"Somebody mind telling me what's going on here?"

I couldn't figure out for the life of me what they were doing alone. Chance grabbed me and told me he would explain everything in the car but Moe disagreed. I wasn't having it any other way, so I jumped in the car, not caring about what she thought. When he told me that they had found Roberto, I was ecstatic. My prayers were answered and I was ready to end his life at that very moment. Without hesitation, I pulled my gun out of my bag and made sure it was loaded.

"Yo, what the fuck Dior? Why do you have that?"
"What you mean?"

"I thought we discussed that you were not carrying that shit around. You want to be Cleo so fucking bad." He knew damn well that I went nowhere without Brittany, so he was tripping for no reason. He yelled at me about my damn gun the whole damn ride. He wanted me to walk around with pepper spray and a taser like I was a little kid. My overgrown ass was too damn hood for all of that and could handle myself better with the heat. Everything happened so fast when we got to Roberto's and he fucked me up with the information he gave me. I was lost with this whole Moe situation and just wanted to find my way. For the moment, I had enjoyed the times that we spent as sisters but now that I knew she was my cousin, it was fucking with me. He really killed something inside of me because it hurt finding out that my mother had lied once again. I had so much on my plate and the fact that my wedding was in less than 48 hours was disturbing. I just wasn't happy going into this. Don't get me wrong; marrying Chance was more than what I wanted, but the timing just wasn't right. Had I known these events were going to take place, I would have never set the date so soon. Dakota had mentioned that he had to talk to me, so I was riding with him, being the sister that I was.

"So, what you needed to talk about?"

He took a pull from the blunt then passed it to me. "I fucked up sis; I need advice."

"Advice about what?"

"Look, don't get mad at me aight. I fucked up and I feel bad enough about the shit."

"Dakota, please stop with the procrastinating."

"I had a slip up and fucked Jasmine. Look, before you get-," I couldn't even let him finish because my anger got the best of me and I backhanded him.

"Aye, what the fuck is wrong with you, girl?"

"NO WHAT THE FUCK IS WRONG WITH YOU BOY? You the reason those bitches out in public acting like they don't have any damn sense. Dakota, you wrong as fuck bro and you know it. Why would you back track and sleep with that damn girl?"

"Man, I said it was a mistake aight. Don't put your got damn hands on me no more Dior, real shit."

"Yeah whatever. So, that's what they were fighting about. So, now what are you going to do because if Bree has any damn sense, she should not take your dog ass back."

"That's a fucked up thing to say but, lucky for you, a part of me don't want her to." The things he was saying was unbelievable. Niggas really ain't shit. True enough, I didn't like Bree at first but she is not a bad person at all. Nor does she deserve his bullshit.

"And you act like your relationship always been peachy."

"Don't try to flip this on my nigga because you fucked up. You are fucked up Cody. Look at the way you treated Moe. Mommy not being around really bruised you and it is sad."

"Fuck Moe. You can trust her, but I can't do it." "What is your issue with her? You can't hold grudges."

"Man, are you going to advise me on what's important or try to be a family therapist?"

"You need to choose who you really want and stop playing with people's feelings. You and Jas evidently feel some type of way for each other and as much as I hate it, I can't stop you from being with who you love. You accepted my situation, so it's only right that I do the same." The truth was that I knew how he was and I didn't want to see Jas hurt. I knew she was good for Cody, but he honestly wasn't good for her. He dropped me back at the house and drove off. The time was nearing where I would become Mrs. McCray.

Jas:

A bitch was still 38 hot with the whole Bree situation. I couldn't believe that lil bitch came for me when it was her man that overstepped his boundaries. It didn't sit well with me that she had the audacity to lay hands on me, like I wasn't bout that life. Dakota had told me all about her putting him out the house and him staying back at his condo. I guess he had really fucked up this time. It had been over two weeks since everything popped off with Carlos and I still had not talked to him. The only thing that had me nervous was the fact that he had to have seen Dakota and I having sex. I really didn't give a fuck but, knowing that nigga, he probably had it recorded. I made a mental note to call Dakota as soon as I got home. I stopped by the grocery store to get spaghetti noodles for dinner tonight. Demi was with Dior, so I didn't have to worry about putting her to sleep and all of that. I was walking down the aisle, minding my business when I saw Carlos' alleged wife.

"Well, if it isn't the home wrecker."

"Move around boo; I don't think you want to get that ass tapped again. I am far from a home wrecker, so watch your fucking mouth."

"You didn't beat shit hoe; you barely even touched me."

"Look bitch, can you just go find you something safe to do. I got shit to do, like be productive, now goodbye." I tried to walk by but she side stepped in front of me. I don't know why bitches wanted to continue to bring the ratchet out of me.

"Little girl, I am not going to tell you again to get the fuck out of my way." I pushed her slightly so that I could get by and she pulled me back by my hair. I swung around and hit her with a right hook. I felt a pair of strong arms grab me and push me behind them.

"Jas, what the fuck you doing fighting? You just think you lil Laila now, I see. Take your ass outside."

"Dakota, what are you even doing here? I was cool until she grabbed me. And you don't run shit, so don't tell me to go any damn where. I came to get spaghetti noodles and that's what I'm going to do."

"Aye, who you?"

"Nigga, who are you? This is between me and the hoe so go on about your business."

"This is my business bald head ass girl. Jasmine, who the fuck is this dust bunny?"

"That's Carlos…"

"I'm Carlos' wife and who are you?"

His face turned red as he turned to face me. "Wife? You fucking a married nigga ma?"

"This sad ass excuse of a woman just came out of nowhere saying they are married. He says they are not married, so I don't know. All I know is I don't even fuck with him but every time she sees me, she feels the need to jump stupid."

"She knew he was married, don't believe the hype."

"I didn't ask you nothing ma, so don't talk to me. I'm talking to my baby mama. Yo Jas, you better not fuck back with that nigga; now, let's go." He grabbed my hand and started pulling me towards the door.

"I am grown. Let my got damn arm go. I can walk just fine."

"I can't believe you messing with a nigga that would even fuck with a bitch that looked like that. The fuck type of animal was she? That broad was shaped like an ice cream cone. Tell that nigga he plays too damn much." I looked back and the alleged wife was standing in the middle of the aisle looking stupid with her arms crossed. We got outside and Dakota sat on the hood of his car and sparked up a blunt.

"Nigga, you sparking that shit up like it's legal. Put that shit out fool."

"Man, half of these niggas on my payroll girl; they ain't fucking with me." I shook my head because I hated that he was so cocky.

"So Jasmine, what's up? Wait, where my baby?"

"She is with your sister and what are you doing here anyway?"

"This is a grocery store, slow ass girl. A nigga gotta have a reason to come here?"

"One, your spoiled ass can't cook, and two, I don't see any groceries so what's really good?" I folded my arms to show him that I was serious. It was no coincidence that he just happened to be at this grocery store at the same time as me.

"Aight, you right. It's some shit going on, so I been having all of y'all followed. I was around the corner picking up my cash when my boy called and told me you were in there arguing with that thing."

"Followed? Dakota, what the fuck? So, what's going on because you ain't said shit?"

"Calm your lil hot ass down. You get into one lil fight and you think you bout that shit for real. I didn't tell nobody because the shit is under control."

"Nigga please, I been beating bitches. Does Dior know what's going on?"

"No and she better not find out." I started walking to my car, and he grabbed me and spun me around.

"Since sis got Demi, how about you give me some of that sweet lil pussy before I go handle this shit I'm dealing with?" He was high as hell and probably didn't know what the hell he was saying. He started kissing on my neck and the rest was history.

Chapter 14

King:

It had been a minute since I went over to Joyce's crib, so I was headed over to chill with them for a minute. She had told me that Cali and Rue were back together, but I didn't have shit to say on that. Me and him were cordial for the most part, but it was all because of the money. Ever since we squashed whatever beef we had, more money was coming in. I pulled up to my mother's house and Chasity was sitting on the porch. The scar on her face was something serious, but she only got what she deserved for that shit she pulled.

"Where everybody at?"

"They in there. What made you come over here?"

"Damn, the fuck is your problem today?"

"I'm sorry bro; I just have a lot on my mind. You ready to get married tomorrow?"

"Ready as I'll ever be. A nigga slick nervous though, I can't even flex."

"I bet. I'm happy for you though, believe it or not. I can't wait until the day I get married."

"It's coming sis. Just make sure he is YOUR man and your man only."

I walked in the house and ma was sitting at the table.

"Well, look who it is."

"I should be saying the same about you. You have a little boyfriend now and your ass be on the go. So, what y'all in here doing?"

"Nothing, I'm about to cook. Your fast ass sister upstairs; she still not talking to me."

"Well, ma, can you blame her? She is grown as hell and lived all her life thinking she had the same dad as me and Chas. You wrong for that and you know it. That's not something you keep from somebody, regardless of how bad it is."

"I know son, but he never wanted to meet her, so I did what I thought was best."

"Well, it wasn't what was best for me." I didn't even see Cali standing there.

"Cali, sit down and let me explain."

"Nah, I'm good. I don't know whether you will tell me the truth or not, so we can leave this where it is. I will say this though; this family ain't shit. I don't know who I can trust anymore. My sister wants to sleep with my boyfriend, my brother is leaving me because he decided to have a baby with his baby mama's sister then fell in love with her, and my mother lied to me my whole life. Don't forget how I was left all alone when I was in jail. With that being said, I am moving out. I can't allow my life to be a big mess any longer. I love the hell out of all of y'all, but I hate y'all at the same time." She turned around and went back upstairs. A nigga been so caught up in my own shit that I never considered how my little sister felt. She was fucked up behind a lot of shit and I hated she was dealing with it alone. I went up to her room and knocked on her door. I didn't get an answer, so I opened it and walked in. She was in her closet packing and I stood behind her.

"Cali, can I holla at you?"

"I'm listening."

"Look, don't ever feel like I'm leaving you just because I'm getting married. You still my little sister and that shit will never change."

"You say that now but you barely come around now. Your life is all about Dior and the kids now; you have no time for me. I just have to accept that."

"Nah, you don't have to accept that because I'm going to change that. I just wish you and Chas-"

"Don't even talk about her around me."

"You can't be like that Cali."

"I can and I am. Fuck her." We talked for a while longer and had a better understanding about a lot of shit. Rue text me and told me to meet him at my club, so I was headed there. I didn't understand why the nigga wanted to meet at my place of business, but I was damn sure about to find out. I pulled up to the club and hopped out. I walked into the club and everything in this bitch was rearranged.

"Yo, what the fuck is this?"

"King?"

Rue and his pops walked up behind me and I grilled the both of them.

"Somebody better explain why my entire club been changed around and they better explain quick."

"Calm down nigga, we going to get this shit back right man. Congrats nigga, you about to be handcuffed to one woman after tomorrow." Three strippers walked up to me and started dancing. I had never seen such beautiful asses in my life. These niggas had thrown me a bachelor party. I couldn't believe it, seeing that me and Rue was only business men.

My security guard walked up to me and told me some nigga named Los wanted to talk to me. I walked over to the bar and it was the nigga that Jas had brought to my house.

"What up?"

"I need to holla at you in private if you got time." This nigga sure picked the wrong time to come talk to me on some other shit. I told Rue I would be right back and told Los to follow me to my office.

"So, what you need to holla at me about?" I looked up and the nigga had a gun pointed in my face. "The fuck you on nigga?"

"Shut up and let me talk. Now, I came to give you a proposition and either you can get with it or die behind it." I laughed at his empty ass threat.

"I am so tired of you niggas running around this bitch playing tough. Now, I know for a fact you didn't bring your scared ass in here to kill me because you know you won't leave this motherfucker alive. So, what is it you really want?"

"You killed my cousin and I feel like you owe me for it. I want 60% of every dime that you make if you want to stay alive. Don't test me nigga because I'm well known in these streets and I can make shit happen. I don't-"

"Who the fuck is your cousin?"

He pushed the gun against my temple. "Marco. You know, your brother?"

"Fuck you and Marco nigga, I'm not giving you shit. You come up in this bitch acting like you going to shoot some. You about to end up just like that nigga, so do what you need to do." A knock came at the door and Rue walked in.

"Now, I know you ain't come fuck with my mans at his celebration party. I paid good money for this shit, so I'll be damned if you kill him before a bad bitch give him a lap dance."

Los shot at Rue and missed and I elbowed him in the side, making him drop his gun. I pulled my gun from my waist and emptied the clip in him. I heard everybody screaming downstairs and ducking for cover. How the fuck am I going to get this body out of here?

Rue:

I had my baby back and a nigga was happy as hell. Since we had been back together, I had been emptying every seed my sack contained, trying to get her pregnant. She told me all about the talk her and her brother had, and I appreciated him for bringing my baby back to life. I appreciated him so much that I decided to throw him a bachelor party. True enough, we wasn't close or no shit like that, but I just wanted to show him my appreciation for bringing in that schmoney and looking out for my baby girl. I requested the top dancers over at Magic City and made it do what it do. I told him meet me at his club because I knew he would be confused as to why I would want him to meet me there. We were just starting to turn up when one of his guards said some nigga wanted to talk to him and, when I saw the nigga, he looked sneaky. I could tell he wasn't coming for the pleasantries so when King took longer than expected, I went to see what the hell was going on. I was shocked when I saw the nigga had a gun at his head. What was even more stupid of the nigga was that he took his gun off the target to shoot at me. That was something you were never supposed to do.

"You aight, nigga? What the fuck was that about?"

"Long ass story and a nigga really ain't trying to get into all that." I called my pops clean-up crew as we headed back down the stairs.

Chance:

As much as I wanted to stay and enjoy the party, my mind just wasn't in it. Tomorrow was the day that I was going to marry the woman of my dreams and I was ready to see her walk down that aisle.

"Aye man, I'm out." As I was about to make my exit, Cody and some nigga with a crazy ass walk made their way in.

"Yo, I know damn well you not about to leave with all this ass in the building. I know we ain't buddy buddy, but a nigga came to celebrate with you. This my nigga, Legs. Legs, you already know who this is." He didn't say too much, just gave me a simple head nod, but I wasn't going to turn up about it. I was definitely used to these niggas being salty.

"What up fam? How the hell they get you in the building?"

"Dior big ass mouth told me to come show love and she told me to tell you to check your got damn phone. She said she was going out."

"The fuck? Headed out where and with who? She don't have no damn friends." I pulled my phone from my pocket and saw that she had called 3 times and sent a text.

Wifey: *That bitch's ass better be round and fat for you not to be answering any of my calls. Don't get fucked up Mr. McCray. Anyways, I'm headed out with Jas, see you when we get home.*

"Chill out man. She went out with Jas. Bree got all the kids."

"Shitt, well pour up then muhfuckas." We turned the club inside out until the sun was peeking. I was so fucked up that my vision was blurred.

"Aight nigga, no more drinks for you. Dior will kill me if your ass don't make it to this wedding; let's go." Rue and Cody helped me to the car and Cody got in. I don't know if I was just fucked up but, out of my peripheral, I could have sworn I saw the nigga Legs mugging a hole through me. I didn't trust homeboy and I was going to let Cody know.

"I will have Jas or Bree come get your car. You turned up a little too hard." He took a blunt from behind his ear and fired it up. That nigga smoked more than me and I could smoke a nigga under the table. He dropped me off at the house and pulled off. I ran in to take a shower and take a quick nap to sober up before the wedding. I set my alarm to wake me up in an hour so that I could get my hair cut. Today was the big day; today was the start of my future.

Chapter 15

Cali:

I had been distant from my mother and sister to keep myself from spazzing. I moved out and moved in with Nyrue until my condo was ready. He wanted me to stay with him, but I just wasn't ready for all of that and I still had not completely trusted him. While Nyrue thought he was in the clear and everything was all good, I still had my guard up. He was taking me over to Joyce's house to get the remainder of my things. Luckily, her and Chasity had already left to go to the wedding. I had finally gotten over not wanting Chance to get married and decided to attend. We pulled up at the house and got out.

"This won't take long; I just have a few more bags."

"Aight, I'm going to help you load them up."

"Ok. So, how was the party last night? You were fucked up."

"Mannn, that shit was lit bae. Your brother was turned up to the max."

"I bet he was. He be real live when his ass on that liquor. I am just happy that everything is all good with the two of you."

"Yeah, he aight." He walked over to me and took my bottom lip into his mouth. We started going at it roughly as he started pulling on my dress.

"Nyrue, we don't have time. The wedding is about to start in another hour and I can't mess up my hair." I had gone and had my locs styled, and it was too pretty for his ass to be pulling it out of place.

"Fuck your hair. Let me just taste it."

"Ok, but you are not getting any ass. I got you later on tonight." I hiked my dress up and laid back. He opened my legs as wide as they would go and kissed the inside of my thighs. "Mm, yes." He stuck his finger in and started a come here motion, attacking my g-spot. He wasted no time diving in the cookie jar, flicking his tongue back and forth. "I'm about to cum." Without a response, I came forcefully in his mouth. He slurped up all of my sweet nectar. My eyes were closed as I tried to get my mind off of the amazing orgasm my body had just endured. By the time I opened my eyes, Nyrue had slid in my tunnel and was slow grinding.

"Fuck Calz. This shit like paradise. I want you to have my baby, Calz."

"Mm, fuck. Ok baby." I put my hands on his waist and guided him in and out as my body went into overdrive. The room was quiet as our bodies intertwined and made its own music. Only skin slapping against one another and moaning could be heard. "Shit, here comes another one."

"Push it all out. I'm about to bust too."

I felt dehydrated as my pussy let go of every fluid my body contained. I felt Nyrue's dick going soft, letting me know that he had

117

emptied his seeds into my tunnel. I was out of breath and tried to get myself together. I looked at the clock and it was 2:37.

"Shit, we are going to be late. Damn it Nyrue." I ran and hopped into the shower to clean myself off. I slid on a thong and threw my dress back on. We grabbed my bags and was headed out the door as Chasity came in.

"What are you doing here?"

"I knew you were here, so I came to talk to you."

"Talk to me about what? I already told your ass I don't have..."

My words got caught in my throat when Chasity pulled a gun from the small of her back.

"Chasity, what are you doing? So, you really going to shoot me?"

"Ah, shut the hell up. You think you are so perfect Cali? Well, you're not."

"Chasity, I-"

"I'm not done. You have always thought you were better than me because you always got the good boys while I got the no good ass niggas. All I wanted was Nyrue to care for me, but he was always too stuck up your ass. Nyrue, did Cali ever tell you she killed your babies?"

"Chasity, would you just shut the fuck up." I inched towards her and she cocked the gun back. "It's your fault that you never

118

found a good nigga. You have always been too busy thottin that nobody could ever take you serious. How could you want Nyrue when he is my man? Always has been. It would have never been you, Chasity."

Nyrue stepped in front of me, in case she tried to pull the trigger. "Chasity, listen man, this ain't what you really want to do."

"How the hell would you know? You could have grown to love me if she wasn't in the picture. You think she is so perfect, but she ain't shit, now move out of the way Nyrue. I have enough bullets for the both of you, if you would rather have it that way. I tried everything to get you out of the picture. Why do you think I stopped answering your calls when you were in jail?"

"You snitched on me to the police?"

"Sure did. I had been watching y'all at the studio and saw him put the drugs in your car. I called in with an anonymous tip. I figured they would send your stuck-up ass away for a few years, but Chance just had to run and fight for you like always."

"You ole jealous ass bitch."

I wasn't thinking clear and pushed Nyrue out of the way, then charged at Chasity. Before I knew it, I was on the floor barely able to breathe. I couldn't believe my own sister had shot me.

"CALI." Chasity ran out of the door and Nyrue ran to my side with his phone in his hand calling 9-1-1.

"Baby, just hold on please. Please Cali, just hold on." I felt my body slipping away from as a tear rolled down my face. The pain

I felt from my sister pulling the trigger was much more painful than the bullet that was launched into my side.

"Nyrue, I-I love..." I felt him putting pressure on the wound as he held me tight.

"Shh. Don't try to talk baby. Just hold on; they are on the way." As those words left his mouth, my eyes became weak.

Dior:

I was getting my make-up done for my big day. If you would have told me two years ago I would be marrying the nigga that my brother wanted to kill, I would have laughed. Me and Chance had come so far and this was the beginning of my happily ever after. Everyone was in attendance, getting beautiful for the special occasion. Cay'leigh and Demi were adorable with their dresses on. I hoped they did good walking with the flowers down the aisle. Christian, Deimo, and Demarri were going to push Carson down the aisle with the rings in a wagon. This day was going to be beautiful. Jasmine, Aubree, and Moe were my bridesmaids. I prayed so hard that Bree and Jasmine were able to pull this off without killing each other. Chance didn't really have groomsmen, so it was really only Dakota. His sister's boyfriend Rue was supposed to be in the wedding, but I didn't know what happened with that. I was just happy everyone had finally come together.

"Dior, it's almost time for you to come out."

"Ok."

My make-up artist made sure to add the finishing touches as my stylist fixed on my dress. I looked in the mirror and couldn't believe how beautiful I looked. I walked down the hall to the double doors that would open and stood there patiently. The music came on and it was show time.

Must not of been paying attention

I stepped right on in it, didn't even notice how deep I was

I went from the ground to the top of the cloud

And now as I look down I see where I fell into your arms

Now I got love all over me

I stepped slowly, sure to stay on rhythm. With each step I took, I felt a butterfly fluttering across my stomach. I looked up and there he was, my King, standing there awaiting the throne for me to join him. I made it to the front and he grabbed my hand to help me up the step. He flipped the veil from out of my face and looked at me. We looked into each other's eyes and I saw my future. I saw the love that he had for me. It caused a tear to escape each of our eyes.

"You look beautiful bae." He wiped the tear out of my eye and bit his bottom lip. We turned toward the pastor as he started to speak.

"We have come together at the invitation of Dior Baker and Chance McCray to celebrate the uniting in Christian love, their hearts and lives. This is possible because of the love God has created in them, through Jesus Christ.

Jesus said, 'I am come that they might have life and that they might have it more abundantly.' This abundant life, for many people, is an impossible dream, yet God wants us all to have this abundant life and proved His love for us by giving His Son, that we might have this life. Is there anyone that truly believes that these two should not be joined in holy matrimony, speak now or forever hold your peace?"

I looked back, daring anyone to try and ruin this moment.

Silence.

"Fair enough." He was about to continue, but a certain somebody stepped forward.

"I do."

"Moe, what the hell are you doing?"

"I'm sorry Dior; I just can't let Chance go through with this."

Dakota cleared his throat. "I told you, Dior. This bitch been plotting since day one. Bitch, you have to be remedial to think you about to fuck up my sister's big day."

Chance grabbed Moe's arm and escorted her to the back. I was pissed and ready to beat her ass. Five minutes later, he came back in but Moe was nowhere in sight. He came and stood beside me, then grabbed my hand.

"Pastor… continue please."

The pastor cleared his throat, then did what he was told. "The bride and groom have prepared wedding vowels. We will start with the groom."

Chance looked me deep into my eyes and spoke to my heart. "Baby, you know I don't know how to really do all this but let me just keep it short. Dior, the day that I met you, I knew that I needed you. You made me want to do better in life. Coming home to you every night was never a want but it was more so a need. I needed you more than I needed to breath. You stole my heart and I never want it back. You mean more to me than any dollar in these streets. You and my kids are the reason I go hard as I do. God showed out when he created you and brought us together, and I will die before I fail him and hurt you. You are my heart bae and I'm happy to be standing here on this very day as you become my wife. Ain't no more street life in it. At the top, it's just us..." He wiped the tears that poured from my eyes. Shit, I had to figure out how to top that.

"Never them. Chance, my king, my love, I truly thank you. I thank you so much for never giving up on me. You rode it out with me when I know it was hard. We have been through so much in such a short time, but I couldn't imagine anyone better to go thru it with. Both of us are far from perfect, but we are perfect for each other. You saw something in me that nobody would have taken the time to look for and that was love. You love me for me and I appreciate more than any word could express. "

"Chance, since it is your intention to marry, join your right hands and declare your consent. Do you take Dior to be your lawful wedded wife, to have and behold from this day on, for better or for worse, for richer or for poorer, in sickness and in health, as long as you both shall live?

"I Do."

"Dior, do you take Chance to be your lawful wedded husband, to have and behold from this day on, for better or for worse, for richer or for poorer, in sickness and in health, as long as you both shall live?"

"I Do."

"You may kiss the bride."

"Ladies and gentlemen, I present to you, Mr. and Mrs. Chance Deshawn McCray." We took a step down as Ms. Joyce jumped up and started screaming.

"MY BABY!" Chance ran to her side and tried to get her to calm down.

"She shot my baby."

"What? Who?"

"Chasity… she shot Cali."

Chapter 16

King:

Just as quick as this became the best day of my life, it had become my worst. It felt like my soul left me when my mother said that Cali had been shot. It hurt even more to know that it was Chasity behind it. When I saw that Cali wasn't at the wedding, I figured she just wasn't able to handle that I was getting married. Under different circumstances, I would have been on a war path to cause mayhem in the city, but I could never kill my sister.

"Baby, I am so sorry, but I have to go check on my sister." Dior just stood there in shock as tears poured from her eyes.

"I completely understand. Let me get changed and I will be there. Is she at Grady?"

"Yeah."

I kissed her then ran out of the door behind my mother. This shit was all bad.

"Who called you?"

"Nyrue is at the hospital with her. How could Chasity do something like this, Chance? She can't hate her sister that much?"

"I don't know ma, but, trust me, I'm going to find out." I was pushing 120 on the dash all the way to Grady. I needed answers and I was determined to get them. I swerved into the parking deck and jumped out, not giving a damn that I was parked illegal. We ran into the hospital and up to the floor that Cali was on. When I got to her floor, Nyrue was sitting in the waiting room with his head in his hands.

"Yo Rue, what the fuck happened?"

"I don't know what the fuck Chasity was on. Me and Cali went by your mom's crib to get the rest of her shit before we came to the wedding and Chasity came in. They had a few words and Chas pulled a gun from behind her back. I jumped in front of Cali, but she charged at Chasity and Chas shot her. Man, I can't lose her, man. I swear, I will go fucking ape shit."

"Calm down. What are they saying?"

"She was shot in her side, but that's all I know so far. They won't give me any more info since I'm not family." I could tell it was fucking with him pretty hard and, at that moment, I saw how much love he had for my sister. I walked up to the nurse's station but they told me to have a seat until the doctor came out. I was so tired of coming to this damn hospital over stupid bullshit. I went to sit back down and Dior came running in with Christian. I felt bad that we had to leave our own damn wedding because Chasity wanted to be stupid.

"Baby, what are they saying?"

"I don't know. I'm about to lose it though, if I don't hear something."

"Family of Cali Frazier?"

Me and my mother jumped up and ran over to the doctor. "Cali was hit in the side and we had to surgically remove it. Luckily, the bullet didn't hit any major organs. She is going to be just fine. You all can see her but it has to be two at a time."

"Come on ma." Me and my mother were headed to the back when Chasity walked in with a tear stained face. Rue's face turned red and full of anger.

"Bitch, you got some nerve bringing your thot ass up in here. You and your jealous ass ways could have caused my baby to lose her life."

"Hold up nigga. I understand you mad, but you not about to disrespect my sister."

"Fuck this man, I will be back later." He stormed off and got on the elevator.

My mother walked up and slapped spit from Chasity's mouth.

"Ma, I am so sorry. I didn't mean to do it, I swear. My finger slipped."

"How could you try and kill your own sister? What if she would have died Chasity?"

"I said I'm sorry. So, she is ok?"

"Yeah, she good. Chas, that was real foul. You saying you made a mistake, but why the fuck would you pull out a gun in the first place? You couldn't have gone there with good intentions if you felt you needed a gun."

"I'm sorry but look at me. Cali always gets what she wants. I already feel ugly and then she goes and makes it worse by slicing up my damn face. Y'all have always taken her side. It's not fair."

"Chasity, I am your mother and I love you. You can't live your life worrying about the next motherfucker." She tried walking towards her, but Chas took a step back.

"I love y'all, I swear I do, but I can't do this anymore. Nobody will ever love me the way I need to be loved." She pulled the gun from out of her purse, cocked it, and put it to her head. "Tell Cali I'm sorry."

Me and my mother jumped towards her and tried to grab the gun, but she pulled the trigger.

"CHASITY NOOO!!!" My sister's brain matter splattered all over us. Fuck, today was a bad day.

Bree:

Everybody was at the reception hall talking and having a good time since it was already paid for. I was missing Dakota something serious, but I would die before I let his ass know. I was done playing with him and his little side bitch. I was shocked that he wasn't even trying to come back home. I guess he ran back to her for comfort. When I saw him dressed down at the funeral, it took everything in me not to snatch his ass up and take him to another room. He was looking good as hell, no lie. It also took everything in me not to beat Jasmine's ass again with her fake ass. I hated that the wedding was stopped because of Chance's sister getting shot, but a part of me didn't sympathize. As evil as it may sound, I wanted him to feel the same pain that I felt when he took my sister away. True enough, it wasn't confirmed that he was behind it, but I knew better. Adore never had problems with nobody to the point they would want her dead. I couldn't even act like I felt sorry for him if I tried.

"Aye Bree, why you just standing there looking retarded?"

"Dakota, please leave me alone. You not on a good enough side to crack jokes so tread lightly."

"Man, whatever. You stay trying to act like you don't miss this good shit. Come on to the house and drop them drawers."

I chuckled lightly because I was slightly tempted. "Boy please, you wish. You will never hit this ass again; better go try that with your bomb bitch of a baby mama."

"Watch out with all the disrespect Bree."

"Ohhh, check you out. You jumping in defense mode; you must be fucking her already."

"Man, whatever, I'm out. You really need to grow the fuck up."

"Bye. I didn't ask your hoe ass to come bother me in the first place. You could take your sons with you, though. They do still exist."

"I know damn well you not trying to turn up like a nigga not taking care of his kids. You really about to get your bald head ass cursed out with your no neck having ass."

I had to laugh at his antics because I had him all in his feelings. I didn't care about that shit though. "Bye Dakota, you are dismissed. I hope your limp ass dick fall off with that dirty ass penis you passing out."

He walked off yelling over his shoulder. "Yeah, yeah, whatever. Shut your musty ass up before I shove it down your loose ass throat."

"What the hell y'all looking at? The show is over." I walked outside to get me some fresh air and then Moe walked up.

"What are you doing back?"

"I came to apologize to Chance and Dior. Are they in there?"

"Nah, they left. Something came up."

"What could have po-"

"Cut the bullshit Moe, what did you really come back for?"

"Damn, why the hell are you so salty?"

"My bad. Dakota just pissed me off."

"Yeah, he is a real asshole."

"Indeed. So, why did you try to stop the wedding?"

"I don't know. I guess it didn't hit me that I still loved him until I saw him at that altar. Chance is the only man that I have ever loved and, once upon a time, I felt like I would be the one to carry his last name."

"Don't we all think that when we are in love? You have to let that go now Moe. He is happy and I know it hurts seeing that, but it is what it is.

"Yeah, you right."

Moe:

I thought that I was over Chance until I saw the way he looked at Dior. That look was all so familiar to me, considering it was the same look he once gave me. With each word the pastor spoke, I felt my heart cracking. I thought that I was doing the right thing, trying to stop the wedding. I guess a part of me felt that he would agree with me and love me again. It was just wishful thinking. I was more than hurt when he put me out and the words that he spoke to me continuously replayed in my head.

"What the hell is your problem making objections at my wedding?"

"Chance, I still love you and I can't help that. Why can't you just come back to me and Christian? I promise I will be better than before."

"I have custody of Christian and I would never come back to you. I love Dior and that is just what it is. Deal with it. I would never leave her for anybody, especially you. You lucky that we even allowed your selfish ass to be a part of this union. I can't believe you tried to pull this bullshit. Get the fuck out."

"Chance, I-"

"Moe, you know how I roll, so don't make me have to ask you again. Now, get the fuck out!"

Yeah, I was hurt, but what did I expect? After careful consideration, I decided to go to the hall and apologize for whatever damage had done. When I pulled up, Bree was standing outside. I walked up to her, wondering why she was outside. She had informed me that Chance and Dior had left because of something that happened, but I didn't want to ask too many questions. I left the hall and sat in my car, thinking about my life. It seemed like life just couldn't get right for me, no matter how positive I tried to stay. I couldn't even get my shit together for my own son's sake. I felt that I had failed, once again, as his mother. At that very moment, I thought about what could possibly be the root of all my problems. I needed to find Carole Baker; I had to find my mother.

Chapter 17

Cody:

It took everything in me not to haul off and slap the shit out of Bree. Her mouth had gotten reckless since we split and I wasn't the nigga for all of that. I understood why she was mad but to kick shit like a nigga wasn't doing for his seeds had me 38. I was very happy for my sister and wished her the best. I know we came a long way from where we started and I knew it was nothing but growth. I felt bad for the nigga King though because it seemed like homie couldn't catch a break. First, his brother tried to kill him, then his sister turns around and shoots the other one. That nigga had a fucked up family. Since me and Bree broke up, I had been spending a lot of time with Jas and was starting to think I chose the wrong one from the jump. Jas was like one of the homies. We played the game together and talked about everything you could think of. She didn't nag a nigga about shit, even though she really didn't have the right anyway. We had been fucking like rabbits since the day I caught her at the grocery store. I realized that I never even gave her the opportunity to be my lady and was seriously considering it. The fact that she was such a great mother to my daughter was a major plus. I saluted both of my baby mamas in that department because I never had to worry about my kids being mistreated.

"What you out here thinking about big head?"

"Life. I thought you left."

"Nah, I was feeding Demi and changing my clothes. You aight?"

"Hell yeah. I was just thinking about us and what it would have been like if we had given it a shot."

"Dakota, what are you talking about? Don't start getting all mushy and shit."

I had never just taken a real look at Jas, but she was beautiful. I don't know why a nigga was all in his feelings nor what had me like this, but I wanted her.

"I'm dead ass Jas. You never thought about how we would have been if we had actually been in a relationship. I don't know what made me treat you like you were just a fuck, when you were always more than that. I have always loved you; I just didn't want to fuck up our friendship."

"Yeah, that used to always cross my mind. I erased all of that when you hurt me though."

"So, what about now? You don't think we should try and at least give Demi a chance at growing up in a two parent home?"

She stood there staring, like she was in deep thought. "Listen Dakota, I don't know about that. When you chose to be with Bree, I let you go. I erased any feelings that I contained concerning you because I felt like we would never be. The first time you came back around and we had sex, it was a mistake. True enough, I know we acted on our feelings, but sex was all it was."

"Damn. So, you can honestly stand here right now and say the past week that we have spent meant absolutely nothing to you?"

She nodded her head, yes, but I knew better. I knew her well enough to know that she didn't mean nothing that she had just said.

"If you tell me right now that you want to stop what we have been doing and just be co-parents, then I will never mention it again."

"Ok."

"Ok what?"

"We can give it a shot. But I don't want no shit Cody. Either you are with me or you with Bree, no back and forth Peter."

"Who the fuck is Peter?"

"Off of Love & Hip Hop. You know how he confused as hell and don't know who he wants? That's you, but the only difference is I will chop your dick off."

"And you will die. This good shit brings the cash in."

"Don't play." She punched me in the arm and we started laughing. Yeah, I made the right decision. Jas is cool. I had a phone call, so she went to get Demi.

"Yo."

"Where you at?"

"Who this?"

"Simone. You deleted my number or something?"

"Shit, your number was never saved ma. What up though?"

"Push up on me; I got something good for you."

"Nah, I'm good on that. What you got good for me? I hope you not talking about that trash between your legs."

"Trash? Why do you keep saying that?"

"Because I'm not lying, that's why. Look ma, take my advice. Stay with your girlfriend, please, because no nigga in his right mind would want that between your legs. Something is not right with it, now be easy." With that said, I hung up before she could respond. I didn't have time for Simone and her trash ass pussy. She should be ashamed to even be trying to toss that shit around. Ugh!

I sparked up a blunt while I stood outside waiting on Jasmine and Demi to come back out. I hoped that everything worked out with Jas because this was it for me and if it didn't, I was going back to the basics.

Cali:

I woke up to Nyrue sitting beside my bed with his head down and my mother sleeping in the chair by the window. I was still in pain but even more happy to be alive. Chasity had really hurt me knowing that she wanted to end my life. I would have never thought that her jealousy went that deep. I lifted my hand and rested it on Nyrue's head to let him know I was up. He looked up and I gave him a faint smile.

"Baby. Ms. Joyce, Cali is up."

"Cali, how you feeling?"

Her eyes were puffy and red, in which I knew she had been crying. "I'm going to be ok ma. I'm sorry for the way I have been acting."

"Shh, no need to apologize. I was wrong on all levels." Her and Nyrue looked at one another, like they had something on their mind.

"Where is Chance? I can't believe I missed his big day."

"He understands baby girl. He went to get something to eat. He should be back in a few." I laid my head back against the pillow and let out a sigh. My body was tired and sore.

"Bae, you scared the shit out of me, ma. I seriously thought that I lost you."

"Has anyone heard from Chasity? I don't want to press charges. We just need to sit down and have a long talk."

"Yes baby. She told me to tell you that she is sorry. Cali, I have something to tell you." My mother's eyes turned glossy as she prepared what she was about to say. She started crying and trying to catch her breath.

"Ma, what is it? Don't cry please."

Nyrue kissed the back of my hand. "Cali, Chas came up here and apologized and then she... she... she killed herself. She shot herself in the head right in the waiting area in front of everybody. I am so sorry bae and I feel like it's all my fault."

It felt like I was blacking out with every word that came out of his mouth. Why would Chasity do this? We could have gotten over all of this.

"Please tell me this is a joke. Chas wouldn't do that. Please tell me she didn't do that."

"I'm sorry Calz, but it's true. Your mother and Chance tried to stop her, but it was too late."

Joyce fell to her knees and let out a gut wrenching scream. "Why? Why my baby?"

It felt like a bad dream that I couldn't wake myself up from. Nyrue ran to my mother's side and hugged her tight. Chance and Dior walked in and he went to help Nyrue get my mother up. Dior walked over to me and grabbed my hand.

"Good to see you again Cali. How you feeling?"

"In pain. I almost lost my life and I will never see my sister again. Why would she do that Dior?"

"I don't know boo. Sometimes people just can't deal with a guilty conscience. She was just going through something we didn't know about."

My heart was aching so badly, and I just wanted to talk to Chas and let her know how much I loved her. I would have hugged her and told her I was sorry. There were so many words left unsaid and I hated the fact that she died without us settling our differences. There was a knock on my room door and in walked a brown skinned man with eyes like mines. He stared me in the face and cracked a smile.

"You are so beautiful. You look just like your sister, Ahsha."

"What the hell are you doing here?"

Nyrue walked over into the unknown man's face. "Y'all know this nigga?"

My mother stepped forward. "Yeah, I know him. Cali, meet your father. What the hell are you doing here?"

"Just because I am not in her life doesn't mean that I don't keep up with her. I was in Miami and got a call saying that she was here, so I came back. Now, I know me coming here may be a problem for you, but I wanted to see my daughter."

"Oh I'm your daughter now? Help me understand because 24 hours ago, I wasn't a damn thing to you." I was mad because it took me damn near losing my life for him to come see me. If that wasn't fucked up, then I didn't know what was.

"You have every right to be mad with me, but your mother is just as much at fault as I am."

"Elaborate please."

My mother had a nervous look in her face, like she didn't want him to say nothing else. "Baby, this is not the place for that. Let's get you healed and then we can discuss everything."

"No, I want the truth now. I will not wait until he escapes again before I get my questions answered."

"When your mother told me she was pregnant, she said it was his father's baby." He pointed at Chance.

"Yes, I should have looked further into it, but I was in love with someone else. I figured she didn't want him to know about us, so I went along with it. When you were born, I saw pictures of you and I knew without a doubt you were mine. Did I come for you? Yes, I looked for you up until you were about five years old. Joyce changed her number and moved y'all to a whole new area. I gave up because I thought I would never find you. I found out where you were when you were about twelve years old. For Christmas, I would send you plenty of money through Chasity. Your mother didn't even know that I was in contact with Chasity because she was too busy brainwashing you into thinking that man was your dad. I am sorry baby girl; please, forgive me."

The look of death was evident on my face. I could literally choke my mother right now. Chance stood there shaking his head, while she stood there looking stupid.

"You just don't know how to tell the truth, do you? It's like the truth is poisonous to you."

"Cali, let me-"

"Fuck that. I don't want to hear anything you have to say. Matter of fact, get out!"

"I am still your mother."

"You are not a mother of mines. Matter of fact, I am dead to you."

Nyrue snapped in my direction. "Cali, don't be like that."

"Whatever. Everybody get out, except for my dad. I need more answers." I put everybody out and was face to face with the man that gave me life. "So, how are you going to fix this?" "I am so sorry for abandoning you. It's more to it than your mother may have told you. When I met your mother, I was engaged to be married. She ended up getting pregnant and I told her I couldn't be there because of my situation. She told me that she knew what to do. She said that she would tell your sibling's father that he was also yours. As bad as it sounds, I ran with it. I am so sorry, how can we make this right?"

As bad as I wanted to stay mad I couldn't. I wanted to know my real father. I wanted love from wherever I could get it. "We will see when I get out of here." With that said he left his number and left. I knew that was the last time I would hear from him.

Chapter 18

Moe:

It had been a week since I had decided to search for my birth mother and I had found three possible matches. The one that I truly believed to be my mother had a house over in Alpharetta and I was headed there. I had searched high and low from Facebook to the ancestor search. I pulled up in front of her house and sat in my car. I was a nervous wreck because I didn't know how this would turn out. *Lord, please let this work in my favor.* I pulled down my vanity mirror and looked at myself, then got out. I checked my appearance through the windows in my car and was satisfied. Each step that I took towards the door, my stomach dropped another inch. I rang the doorbell twice and stepped back to get my composure together.

"Who is it?"

Silence. Calm down Monique, calm down.

I was sweating bullets. I was angry with my mother but still wanted to get to know her. I needed answers.

A little girl that looked to be about 14 years old opened the door and looked me up and down.

"Yes?" She was so beautiful, but it was crazy because I saw a slight resemblance.

"Umm, is Carole home?"

"MOM, SOMEBODY IS AT THE DOOR FOR YOU!" She stood there staring at me as if she felt the same thing I was feeling. An older woman came down the stairs carrying a laundry basket. She sat the basket down and walked over to me.

"You here for my daughter?"

"Yes ma'am."

"She will be down in a second. You can come in and have a seat." I walked in and sat down on the couch and patiently waited. The house had a nice décor and everything was so neat. There was a white room when you walk in to the left and an accent room across from it. I was admiring the pictures on the wall when I heard someone coming down the stairs.

"Who was at the..." I stood up and started walking towards her and she did the same.

"Mo...ni...que? Is that you?" Her eyes started to water as I shook my head yes. "How did you find me?" As bad as I wanted this moment to be a happy one, I needed the answers of why she threw me away, more so why she never came for me.

"I need you to answer a few things."

She nodded her head as we retreated back to the couch. The girl that answered the door came and stood in the doorway.

"Let me explain everything please."

"I'm listening."

"I was only 16 when I got pregnant with you and I panicked. When I told my mother that I was pregnant, she threatened to disown me because you were conceived with the deacon from her church. I didn't know what to do because I had no means of taking care of you. Your uncle Roberto, who I assume you met, was with your aunt Shan at the time. Me and Shan were the best of friends, so close that we made a pregnancy pact. We carried you and your cousin full-term and went into labor the same day. Unfortunately, your cousin didn't make it and it devastated her. When I was released from the hospital, I went home to my parents, but they wouldn't welcome me like I thought they would. She told me if I wanted to have a place to live, I had to get rid of you. I couldn't bring myself to do it, so I left that day. I wasn't surviving because no one would hire me. Shan eventually stopped talking to me and Roberto grew distant. I later learned that she wanted him to kill me and raise you as her own. I knew the power that she held, so I protected you by giving you to child protective services. Trust me when I tell you that I have been searching high and low for you since I turned 18. Monique, I am so sorry."

Both of our faces were full of tears and I was speechless. I didn't know whether I should be mad or forgive her. "You don't know how fucked up my life has been. I was molested in every home those bastards sent me to. I have gotten pregnant more times than I could count because I was forced to sleep with men for money. Carole, I have wanted to hurt myself so many times because I felt nobody loved me."

"I'm sorry baby, please forgive me."

I wanted to stay mad, I really did, but this was something I had been wanting all my life. She was open to have me as her daughter and that's all that mattered. "I forgive you."

"Thank you so much. I promise, from this day forward, I will be the best mother I can be. Do I have any grandbabies?"

"Yes, you have one. He is 5 and his name is Christian."

She motioned for the girl from earlier to come over and she did. I was so caught up in our personal therapy session that I had forgotten she was there.

"Monay, this is your older sister Monique. Monique, this is Monay. Monay is 16."

She stuck her hand out for me to shake it, but I grabbed her into a hug. I didn't want to be mad about anything anymore. I had my biological mother back and I wanted to seize this moment.

Dior:

"Ooh baby, circle right there."

"Right here?"

"Mm. Yes." I was enjoying every minute of being Mrs. McCray. Even though our wedding day had pretty much been ruined, we were making up for it every day since.

"Shit, this shit too sweet." He stood up, stroking his manhood while licking his lips. My husband was so fucking sexy. He slid into my love tunnel and grinded slowly. I put my hands on the headboard and wrapped my legs around his waist, then started riding him from the bottom.

"Mm. This pussy feel good bae?"

"You already know. Shit."

"Fuck me harder."

He did as he was told and started pounding into my juice box. I didn't want him to outdo me, so I started throwing it back even harder. He slowed down and took one of my breasts in his mouth. I bit down on my bottom lip to distract myself from the pleasurable pain he was delivering.

"I love the fuck out of you, girl."

"Mm. I love... you... too." My eyes were rolling to the back of my head as he was swerving his hips, hitting my spot. When I felt his body loosen up, I rolled over, landing on top. I slid back down on his dick and started riding him with no mercy. I leaned forward with my hands on his chest and started bouncing my ass up and down. He grabbed ahold of my waist and slowed me down.

"Slow down baby. I'm not trying to bust yet."

I turned my body around and grabbed ahold of his ankles and started riding reverse cowgirl position. "Ooh, daddy. Here comes a big one." My juices flowed rapidly and saturated his entire pole. I came so hard that it was all over his stomach.

He slapped me on the ass and pushed me forward so that my hands were on the floor and he was on his knees. He stuck his thumb in my ass and started massaging my hole. "Oh my God. I'm about to cum again."

He bent down and nibbled on my ass cheek as he pounded my pussy from the back. I felt his dick jerking as he emptied his seeds in me. I fell forward, landing on the floor, and he fell on the bed. I couldn't move; I knew I was stuck. After that session, I was sure I had no energy. "Damn girl. Your ass going to be pregnant again."

"Don't say that; we have enough."

"Shittin me. We got 3 more to go."

"Whatever." I laid there for about ten minutes until I built up the strength to get up. Chance was on the bed snoring butt ass naked. I threw the sheet over him, then went to get in the shower. I had to go pick the kids up from Jas' house and find them something to wear for tomorrow. Chasity's funeral was tomorrow and I was far from ready for it. Cali was home, but she wasn't the same. Ms. Joyce had completely shut the world out. I understood it though because she was dealing with a lot. Chance was trying to be strong, but I knew he would break down tomorrow. The entire situation was just fucked up. I got out of the shower and wrapped myself in a towel. I turned on my Chi irons so that I could press out my hair. I came out of the bathroom and Chance was standing there biting on his lip. He picked me up and sat back on the bed. I straddled him and he loosened the towel. "No Chance, I have to go get the kids."

"Man, they aight. Did she call you and say you had to pick them up?"

"No, but you know I have to find them something to wear. Why you so damn horny all the time?"

"You possess that crack girl; I'm addicted. Why else you think I married you?" He burst out laughing and I punched him in the chest.

"That's not funny nigga, move." I stood up and went into my panty drawer. I grabbed a pair of lace boy shorts and the matching bra and put them on. I went into the closet and got a pair of joggers and a Nike shirt. I slid on my Nike flip flops, then went back into the bathroom. I did a quick press to my hair and exited the bathroom. I grabbed my MCM backpack and headed out.

"Alright babe, I will see you in a few."

"Aight, be careful. Love you."

"Love you too. Oh and where are the keys to your old school?"

"Oh hell nah, you not driving that."

"Why not?"

"The hell is you doing?" He stood up and walked me down the stairs.

"Because you not about to wreck my shit. That's for grown ass men, not little ass women."

"Boy bye. Where them damn keys?"

"I'm serious Dior, no. It's two other cars you can drive, pick one."

"Ugh, you make my ass itch. Give me the keys to the Challenger then."

He gave me the keys and I walked outside. I started the engine and looked for a song to play. I found his Kevin Gates Islah album and turned to "2 Phones." I sparked a blunt and pulled out of the driveway, bopping my head to the music.

I got two phones, one for the plug and one for the load

I got two phones, one for the bitches and one for the dough

Think I need two more, line bumpin' I'm ring, ring, ringin'

Countin' money while they ring, ring, ringin'

Trap jumpin' I'm ring, ring, ringin'

I pulled up at Jas' house and her, Cody, and the kids were outside. I found that quite weird, considering the fact that a couple of weeks ago they hated each other. I got out of the car and walked over to them, and they both were looking nervous.

"What the hell y'all looking like that for?"

"Nothing," they both said in unison.

"Hmm, I bet. So Cody, what you doing over here?"

"This damn near my crib and I came to spend time with my girls."

"Girls is plural; you aware of that, right?"

"Yeah Dior, damn. I know what the fuck I said. They are my girls. Me and Jas are together."

She was sitting there like a lost damn puppy. "Dakota, you are one confused ass nigga."

I was sick of all three of their ass.

Chapter 19

Jas:

I was trying this relationship shit out with Dakota and, so far, everything was going good. It seemed like Carlos had just dropped off the face of the earth because I had not heard from him. It was even more weird that his phone was off. I knew that he had not changed his number because he did all of his business on that phone. Dakota was spending a lot of time at my house and every moment of it was priceless.

"What we eating tonight? A nigga hungry as fuck."

"I got a full course meal right here, and it's hot and ready like Lil Caesars."

"Girl, don't nobody want that hot ass pussy. You didn't even wash that shit today. Bye Felicia."

"I swear, I can't stand your petty ass."

"Nah for real, come sit that hot pussy on this long dick and let me be the judge."

I did as I was told and walked over to him and straddled him. He lifted my shirt and took my nipple in his mouth and started nibbling on it. "Mm. Baby."

"Aye, for real though, we gotta stop fucking like rabbits or your ass going to be pregnant again." As if he hadn't just made that mini speech, he stuck my breast back in his mouth. While he was sucking my breasts, I started kissing him on his neck. "Fuck, girl."

He flipped me and laid me down on the couch and pulled my boy shorts down. He took off his pants and boxers, then slid in it with no warning. I started playing with my clit as he grinded into my body with a slow rhythm.

"Shit, fuck this pussy daddy."

"I damn sure will. This shit feel like heaven." I started contracting my pussy muscles, squeezing the life from him each time he tried to pull out. My pussy was a vacuum cleaner as it sucked him back in. "Shit, stop doing that shit Jas. You going to make a nigga bust."

I reached down and grabbed ahold of his balls and started massaging them each time his dick exited my love tunnel. He leaned toward my ear and whispered, "I'm glad I chose you. I love you, girl."

"Mm. I love you too baby. Fuck me harder." He stood up and grabbed me while I wrapped my legs around his waist. He lifted me up with my legs around his neck and dove in. He was circling his tongue and my body felt as if it went through an electric shock. "Shit baby, that's right. Make this pussy cum." He lowered me down and slammed me against the wall and continued to plunge into what was rightfully his. I felt my juices leaking as they left my milk and honey all over his shaft.

"I'm about to bust baby."

"Ooh, shit, me too. Give me one sec." My legs started trembling as our bodily fluids collided with one another. He let me down and smacked me on the ass.

"Girl, that's that snapper right there. Got damn."

I pecked him on the lips, then ran upstairs to hop in the shower before I prepared dinner. I made it up the stairs and turned the hot water on, as hot as I could take it. I grabbed my Cherry Blossom body wash and put my phone into the loud speaker then stepped in. Bryson Tiller's single "Exchange" came through the loud speaker.

This what happen when I think about you

I get in my feelings, yeah

I start reminiscing, yeah

Next time around, fuck I want it to be different, yeah

Waiting on a sign, guess it's time for a different prayer

Lord please save her for me, do this one favor for me

I had to change my play of ways got way too complicated for me

I was in the shower twirling my hips when I felt a wet rag slap my ass. "OUCHHHH!" Dakota stood there laughing and stroking his pole. "Why do you have to play so much?"

"Damn baby, you ain't never gave a nigga a lap dance. That ass looked good moving like that. Make that thang clap for me one time." I turned around and started clapping my ass; he pushed me into the wall and rammed his dick in me from the back.

"Shit Dakota, my hair."

"I'll buy you a new weave." He was pounding me from the back. He pushed an arch further into my back with one hand while massaging my nipple with the other.

"Lawd, mm."

"Feel good baby?" *Smack.*

"Yes. Ooh, it's in my stomach."

"Good. Now clap that ass on this dick like you just did."

I clapped my ass like he told me, then made my ass cheeks jump. My hair was soaking wet because we were having sex directly under the shower head.

"Baby, she about to… explode."

"Tell her go ahead then." He pulled out and picked me up against the wall and licked every ounce that my body released.

We washed each other off and got out of the tub. Thank God Demi was still sleeping because the way I was screaming, I was sure that she would wake up. I was dog ass tired and my legs were sore as fuck.

"You not getting any more ass this week. My coochie is sore as hell."

"I bet I will be sliding in that thang tomorrow. I will let her rest tonight; now, go cook me something to eat. My appetite got bigger."

"I don't know why."

I went downstairs and cooked dinner and for dessert, he feasted on me.

King:

"You feeling alright?"

"Yeah, I'm managing. I just wish things were different."

"It's going to be ok sis. You can stay home if you want."

"Nah, I will be ok." Cali pulled her Chanel shades over her face as we headed to the car. Today was the last day I would see Chasity. We were headed to her funeral and I was at my wit's end with being strong. I had been trying to hold myself together for the sake of Cali and my mother, but a nigga was on the verge of breaking down. We got into the limo and led the line. Dior and the kids were in the car behind us, headed to the church.

"I don't know if I can do this y'all."

"It's going to be ok ma. I got y'all, I promise." Did I really have them though? I couldn't imagine what she was going through losing a child, her youngest child at that. Chasity's death had really taken a toll on my mom and I knew she would never be the same.

We pulled up to the church and I was shocked at how packed it was. I never thought my sister was this loved. Cali got out of the car behind me and waved at the crowd of people as they called her name. I assumed they were peers from their school. We lined up first and walked in to view her body in the casket. I was walking behind my mother and Cali, and it felt like my legs were giving out. How could my sister do this to herself? Pain repeatedly seeped through my soul as my legs grew weaker. Dior walked up and grabbed my hand. I swear she kept me on my toes. After everybody was seated, the Pastor started speaking. It was so crowded that there were a lot of people standing against the wall.

"We are here today to pay our tribute and our respect to our sister, daughter, and friend, Chasity McCray. We are here today to show our love and support for Chasity. To know Chasity was to love her and to love her was to comfort Chasity's family through this trying time. Not only have we dwelled on our own personal feelings of loss over her passing, but our hearts have been drawn toward them. We are also here today to seek and receive comfort. We would be less than honest if we said that our hearts have not ached over this situation. We are not too proud to acknowledge that we have come here today trusting that God would minister to our hearts and give us strength as we continue in our walk with Him. It is our human nature to want to understand everything now, but TRUST requires that we lean and rely heavily on God, even when things seem unclear."

Proverbs 3:5

5 Trust in the LORD with all thine heart; and lean not unto thine own understanding.

"The family has asked for a 3-minute remark session for anyone that would like to share any memories and special moments with Ms. McCray."

I looked around and everybody was doing the same. Cali stood up and made her way to the front. I stood up to walk with her, but she motioned for me to sit back down.

"I'm fine Chance," she said, slightly above a whisper.

She stepped in front of the microphone and cleared her throat. Immediately, her eyes developed a glare as she tried to pull it together.

"Umm, as you all may know, my name is Cali and I was Chasity's sister. I could get up here and be mad, but my heart won't allow me to do that. Growing up, me and my sister were thick as thieves. There was never a time that you would catch one without the other; we were just that close. As the years passed us by, for some reason, Chasity grew distant. She started giving me attitude often and I never understood why. Most of the time, I ignored it. I don't know if everyone here is aware of the events that have taken place, but the truth of the matter…"

She froze up as the tears started pouring from her eyes. I attempted to stand up, but Rue walked up and grabbed my arm. "I got it bro." He walked over and went to stand by Cali. He rubbed Cali on the back as she continued to speak.

"The matters that took place but Chasity… Chasity tried to kill me. Before she shot me, she basically told me she had been

157

jealous of me our whole life. Before she killed herself, she apologized, but I never got the chance to respond. Right here and right now, I want to tell you that I forgive you, Chasity, and I wish we could have talked about it." She wiped her eyes and took Rue's hand as they made their way back to their seats. My mother was sitting there rocking back and forth, crying and pleading for her to come back. After the eulogy, we left the funeral and went to the burial site and shit got real. As soon as they started to lower the body into the ground, Joyce lost it.

"NOO, PLEASE GIVE HER BACK. CHASITY BABY WAKE UP!"

I grabbed one of her arms and Rue grabbed the other. She was fighting trying to get loose, but I wasn't having it. Cali just stood there stuck, like she was lost and trying to find her way.

"This is all my fault."

"Don't say that Cali. How is it your fault? Don't blame yourself for what your sister did ma. You going to stress yourself out."

We threw the flowers on top of the casket and went back to our cars. This was a hard ass pill to swallow. "Fly High Chas."

Chapter 20

Moe:

My life had done a complete 360 ever since I met my mother. We had become quite close since the day we met. We spent our days catching up on old times and bonding. She was like a breath of fresh air and I was more than happy to have found her. She had told me all about her mother telling her that Roberto was murdered but, of course, I didn't give a fuck since I knew that already. The only thing that was missing in my life was that I still didn't have my son to embark on this journey. I had yet to talk to Dior and Chance because all of my calls went unanswered. Carole was riding with me over to their house to give my apologies for the incident at their wedding and so she could meet her grandson.

"So, what type of people are Shan's children?"

"Dior is ok. I'm not sure how to feel about Dakota."

"They are twins, right? Why do you say that?"

"Yeah and he is such an asshole. I mean, he is very rude."

"Oh Lord. I don't need my pepper spray, do I? Ain't nobody got time for that."

"Nah, I hope not. Maybe he will have some manners, who knows?"

We pulled into their driveway and got out. I could only pray that this visit was a pleasant one, seeing that I know they hated me. I rang the doorbell and waited for an answer. The door swung open and there stood Dior with an evil scowl on her face.

"What the hell are you doing here?"

"I came to talk to you and let you meet somebody." She sized my mother up and down and stepped to the side for us to enter. We all went into the living room where the kids were and sat down.

"MOMMY. Where have you been mommy?"

"Hey baby. Mommy has been getting herself together. Why don't you take your sister upstairs while I talk to Mommy Dior?"

"Ok mommy. Come on Cayleigh." I waited until they got upstairs to start talking.

"Okay, first and foremost, I wanted to say I am so sorry for the stunt I pulled at the wedding. I don't know what came over me and I am sorry, Dior. I guess I just got in my feelings. Second, I want to introduce you to my mother, Carole. Carole, this is Dior."

"Wow, you are beautiful. You look just like Shan."

"Thanks but I'm not hear for all that. Moe, why would you do something like that when I learned to trust you? You really hurt me. I have the right mind to beat your ass right now, but I will save that for another day unless I have a change of heart."

"I said I was in my feelings. Please forgive me so that we can move forward and get back to where we were. I know my place and I accept it." Carole sat there in utter shock as Dior looked back and forth between us. I wouldn't blame her if she never forgave me, but it was worth a try.

"I really have to give it some thought. One thing I know and need you to understand is Chance is not just my boyfriend anymore. He is my husband and we are not going anywhere. I need you to understand that this shit is forever until the wheels fall off. Even then, it will continue because we will get to walking. In other words, don't every try that bullshit again. You had your chance at a happily ever after with him and you blew it."

"Understood."

"Good. Now Carole, it is nice to meet you but you have some explaining to do also."

My mother ran everything down to Dior that she told me and by the time she was done, Dior was sitting there holding her chest and shaking her head.

"That is fucked up. My mother was more of a monster than I thought."

"Indeed. Anyway Dior, I wanted to know if we could take Christian for a few hours so that they could bond a little. If you want, I will take Cayleigh also."

"Sure, I don't mind, but let me check with Chance first." She called Chance and he gave us the ok to take the kids out for a few. I was more than happy to spend time with them both. I buckled Christian in the car and Cayleigh in her, seat then headed to Kids

Planet for a fun day. We pulled up to Kids Planet and the kids started screaming from excitement.

"Mommy, mommy, yayy!"

Him calling me mommy warmed my heart and I loved every second. We were in Kids Planet having a great time when an unknown number called my phone.

"Hello?"

"Yes, is this Moe?"

"This is she, who am I speaking with?"

"This is Bree. Are you busy?"

"No but how did you get my number?"

"Dior gave it to me. I need to speak with you whenever you get a chance."

"About what?" Something was weird about this conversation, considering we never held a real conversation.

"I need your help with something and I figured you were the perfect person for it."

"For what?"

"Revenge."

Cali:

I was beyond messed up from losing my sister. I knew we were not on the best terms, but I wished I could take it all back. I loved her through her flaws and didn't understand why things had to end the way they did. Nyrue had been by my side through the entire ordeal and I was more than grateful. I had a follow-up appointment so that the doctor could check on my wound and make sure it was healing properly. God had really showed favor and spared my life. After I left there, I had an appointment to switch forms of birth control at the OBGYN. Nyrue thought that I was getting off birth control, but that wasn't the case at all. I just wasn't ready to take that step in my life yet and wished he would understand.

I left the doctor and headed straight to the OBGYN. I called Nyrue to see what he was doing later on.

"Yo."

"What I tell you about answering the phone like that?

"And when you told me, didn't I tell you this my phone?" He started laughing.

"I can't stand your smart mouth ass. I was calling to tell you the doctor said my wound is healing good and I'm on my way to the OBGYN."

"Aight, that's cool. That's good news right there. I'm headed to the studio; call me when you leave there."

"Ok, I want you to meet me later so that I can treat you to dinner."

"Aww shit, look at you trying to cater to your man."

"My man has been very good to me lately, so how could I not?"

163

"Aight baby, hit my line when you done."

I pulled up to the doctor's office and went inside. I didn't have to wait long at all and was immediately taken to the back. She gave me a cup for a urinary sample and, after that, I waited for the doctor.

"Well, hey Cali, how are you?"

"I'm ok and you?"

"Good. So what brings you in today?"

"I came to switch my birth control. I would like to try the Nexplanon." She stood there staring at me with a slight smirk on her face and it was pissing me off.

"Umm, what are you smiling at?"

"We can't switch the contraceptive sweet heart, I'm sorry."

"What why? You know what, never mind. Just give me my shot then."

"I'm afraid I can't do that either."

"What the hell? Is something wrong with my insurance. What is the problem?"

"Ms. Frazier, you are pregnant."

"Pregnant? How the hell can I be pregnant when I have been on the shot? Something has to be wrong with the test because that is impossible."

"No ma'am. You are very much pregnant. In fact, it took your test no time to read it."

"What the fuck?" I got all of my paperwork and my prescription for my prenatal vitamins. I couldn't believe this shit was happening to me. Why now? How was I pregnant and I had been shot damn near in the stomach? I couldn't be happy right now because I just wasn't ready. I was going to have to get ready though because I was not getting another abortion. This was just my time. I called Nyrue and told him to meet me at Kiku's over on Camp Creek. I knew more than anything that he was going to be more than excited. *Lord, you really hit me with this one.* As soon as those thoughts exited my brain, I opened my car door and started throwing up all over the place. I saw Nyrue parking his car and he hurried and ran over to me.

"Bae, what the fuck? You aight?"

"Yeah, I'm fine." I was far from fine though. I had gotten sick out of nowhere.

"You want to go home?"

"No, I am hungry. I will be fine. I just need to put something on my stomach." I cleaned myself off and he grabbed my hand, leading me inside. We sat at the table and ordered drinks.

"So bae, what did they say at the doctor?" I didn't feel like beating around the bush, so I just let it all out.

"I am pregnant Nyrue." A huge smile crept onto his face as he lowered his hand down to my stomach.

"Baby, you having my baby? Aww man, you having my seed."

I smiled and caressed his face with my hand. "Yeah baby, I am."

"Man, you just made my day, I swear. We gotta get married now."

"I know that's not your proposal?"

"Man, fuck Calz. I'm happy as fuck right now. I feel like I just hit the lotto. Can't nothing top this."

He was the happiest I had ever seen him. I was ecstatic to be the reason behind that smile I loved so much. Nyrue had been the man of my dreams from day one and it made me feel better that he felt this way. He grabbed both sides of my face and rained kisses all over it.

"Baby, a nigga feeling good ma, you just don't know. I got you for whatever and that's my word. I want us to raise this baby together. I love you even more than ever because you carrying my seed."

"I love you too baby." The chef came and cooked our food and we ate. After we left the restaurant, we went to Piedmont Park and walked around. This man was my king, my best friend, and the love of my life. What other man would I want to be the father of my child? At this moment, everything seemed perfect. I just wished that Chasity was here. I wouldn't care about the attitude, if only for a second I had her back.

"What you thinking about babe?"

"Nothing. I was just wishing Chas could have been here for this. I believe she would have been happy for this, at least."

"She sees everything going on. She actually knew you were pregnant before you did. Don't stress yourself babe; she's in a better place."

"I know it. It just hurts, you know?"

"Yeah, I know." We walked thru the park until the wee hours of the night and then went home. We made love all night until the sunrise. My life felt so complete.

Chapter 21

Dior:

To say I was shocked at Moe coming to my doorstep would be an understatement. I was even more shocked that her mother was with her. What made my stomach twist was the fact that she looked like a female version of my disgusting ass father. I knew I would eventually forgive Moe, but I also knew it would take time. Chance was slowly getting back to his old self and I was grateful for that. He had not been the same since the funeral, but I didn't nag him because I understood it. Jas and Dakota had the kids for the weekend, so I was planning a special night for us. For dinner, I prepared teriyaki glazed salmon over rice pilaf with brussel sprouts. I showered before cooking, so I went and threw on a Venice lace teddy with the garter. I lit candles and put rose petals all over the house. I saw bright lights in the driveway, meaning he was home. Luckily, I had just got done setting the table. I hurried and poured each of us a glass of Armand de Brignac "Ace of Spades" Rose. I stood in front of the door holding both glasses as he entered. He walked in and I swear I saw all 32 teeth because he was smiling so hard.

"Damn bae, like that?"

"Here daddy." I handed him a glass while grabbing his other hand, leading him to the table.

"Sit down baby, let me be good to you."

"Word? You did all this for a nigga?"

"You haven't seen the finale yet." I took his shoes off of his feet and tossed them to the side. I took his chain from around his neck and sat it on the island.

"Go ahead and eat baby." He started attacking the food on his plate like he hadn't ate in days. I ate my food while watching him. When we were finish, I took our plates and sat them in the sink. He walked up from behind and started kissing me slowly on my shoulders to the nape of my neck. "Mm, baby wait." I turned facing him and kissed him passionately. I pulled back because I didn't want to ruin my plan.

"Ok babe, give me 5 minutes and meet me in the basement."

"What you got going on?"

"You will see. Five minutes, ok?"

I ran downstairs and started to prepare myself for what was to come. I changed the lightbulb to a red one to give off a passionate vibe. Four minutes later, I heard the door to the basement creep open, so I turned the music on and got in position. I had placed a stripper pole in the basement just for tonight.

I still taste you on my lips, yeah I do

Last night we made love 'til the Sun came

I know it's hard when I leave, I'm not with you

But when I'm gone, holed it down, you're my love thing

You be doin' it, that one and two, that four thing

Let's slow it down a bit, I'll hit you with that foreplay

169

Hop on top, I start to ride you, that's that horseplay

Strip for my baby, bitch we ballin', that's that sports play

I love you, I love you

I had on my 508 Dancer Ellie heels. Chance stopped at the last stair while I swung my hair and twirled around the pole. I have secretly been taking pole classes and learned a few tricks. I climbed the pole and flipped upside down and started clapping my ass cheeks. I twirled my body so that I would land on my feet as I made it to the bottom. I climbed back up and started gyrating my body like I was riding the pole. I climbed the invisible stairs while motioning for him to come here. He slowly walked over as I came down into a split in front of him. He was a few inches away, so I crawled to him and started unbuckling his pants. As soon as I had them down, I wasted no time taking him into my mouth. I stroked his shaft while bobbing my head slowly to the music.

"Shit baby. Suck that shit just like that." I released him, then bent down and juggled his balls in my mouth. I was never one to neglect the balls. I took him back into my mouth, easing every inch down my throat. I started humming to the music as I massaged his nuts. He jerked back and grabbed me, then threw me on the couch in one swift motion. He was like the Hulk as he ripped my teddy off of my body. He plunged into my pussy before I could say anything.

"Ooh, Ch... a... nce. Right there."

"Right here?" The pleasure was too good for me to respond, so I nodded my head.

"Shit girl. I need her to rain on me."

"O...k..." I contracted my muscles as I rode the wave his body took me on. The sweet sounds of us making love was beautiful and relaxing. I saturated his dick with my juices as he nibbled on my ear.

"That's a good girl." While nibbling on my ear, he whispered, "I want another baby Dior."

I shook my head no but I knew he would have his way. He turned me on my side and lifted one of my legs so that he was between them. Our bodies were intertwined with one another as he caused back to back orgasms. He sat up, then flipped me on all fours while yanking me back by my hair. He rammed into my tunnel and started putting the pound game on me. He had my hair pulled back with one hand while choking me from behind with the other.

"Baby... I... can't take it."

"Yes, you can. Fuck. Hold on, I'm almost there." He was circling in my pussy as he sped up. I started throwing it back, then he grabbed both of my arms and pulled them back towards him. I had never experienced a pain so good.

"Baby, I'm about to cum."

"Me too." Our fluids met each other halfway and we both collapsed. Not even two minutes after we collapsed, were we knocked out.

Rue:

I don't think there is a word in the vocabulary that would justify how happy a nigga is that my baby carrying my seed. I had been waiting for this moment for a long time and now that it was here, there was no leaving. That was the reason I had been planning such a romantic day for us. I had already told my pops and the rest of the fam about the new addition, and they were just as excited.

"Calz, are you ready?"

"Yes, here I come."

She came out of the room and her beauty pulled at my heart's strings. She looked amazing. She had on an all-white evening gown and her dreads were styled to perfection. Her make-up was flawless. No lie, I shed real nigga tears. This moment was definitely one to remember. She was 11 weeks and had a small pudge, since she was so little.

"Baby, you look amazing. You see you got a nigga shedding tears and shit. I look lame as fuck huh?"

"No silly, you are just fine." She took her finger and wiped my eye. I took her hand and kissed the back of it. "So, where are we going?"

"You are about to see." We walked outside and I helped her get in. About twenty minutes later, we were at Aria restaurant and went in. I had already made reservations, so I gave them my name and we were seated.

"Calz, I can't stop staring at you, ma. You just look so fucking beautiful and that glow sets your beauty off. I love you, bae."

"I love you too babe! I know that I haven't been the best girlfriend lately, but I appreciate you for being patient with me. You see front row that this baby is kicking my ass."

"Hell yeah, but it will all be worth it in the end."

"Yeah, I know it." The waitress brought back our drinks and took our orders. I was ready for the real show to get started. I shot King a text to see what he had going on. About thirty minutes later, our waitress brought our food out and we ate. I told the waitress to grab our tab and sent the text I had been waiting to send off. Cali was drinking a sip of her water when King, Dior, and their three kids walked in.

"What are you guys doing here?" As if on cue, the restaurant softly played Jagged Edge's single "Let's Get Married."

King and Dior stepped to the side and their kid's shirts read Will You Marry Me?

Cali's eyes watered as she placed her hands over her mouth. I reached into my pocket and got down on one knee. I pulled out the custom 1-carat princess cut diamond ring. What was so special about it was that under the main diamond was a small picture of Chasity that you could see whenever the light hit it.

"Calz, we have been through a hell of a lot, but you remained solid. You have done shit for me that I couldn't even pay my own family to do and that right there means more than you would ever know. The day I met you, I told myself that making you my wife one day would be my priority and I plan on doing just that. I don't want to raise my seed as boyfriend and girlfriend; we too old for that. The only way I see it is with the both of you carrying my last name. When we had that little bump in the road, I lost a piece of me. My breathing pattern was off because a piece of my heart had been ripped. I never want to experience that again so with that being said, will you marry a thoroughbred nigga or what?"

"Y'all and these hood ass proposals," Dior said, causing everybody near us to laugh.

"Yes, yes I'll marry you. I wouldn't have it any other way." I stood up and kissed her. The way we kissed was one that meant we would never let each other go.

King grabbed me into a brotherly hug. "Congrats my nigga, take care of her. Good luck man, but she's your problem now." I gave Dior a hug and thanked them both.

"I really appreciate it y'all. Good looking out King."

I walked over and thanked the manager of the restaurant for making this night happen. I grabbed Cali and we left the restaurant. We cruised through the city listening to slow jams and just enjoying life. She would never know nor understand how good she made a nigga feel tonight, but I would be sure to thank her every chance I got. There wasn't any amount of money that could make me hate this moment. We pulled up to my parents' spot in Buckhead. I was excited to tell them the news.

"Yo, where y'all at?"

"In the office."

I grabbed Cali's hand as we walked in and stood face to face with my parents.

"SHE SAID YES." My mother walked up and grabbed Cali and hugged her.

"Congratulations baby girl. Looks like we have a wedding and baby shower to plan." We stayed over my parents' house talking about the bay and the wedding. The smile on my baby's face was priceless and it warmed my soul knowing that I was the reason for that smile.

"I'm sleepy Nyrue, you about ready?"

"Yeah, let's bounce." I hugged and kissed them goodbye and we got into the car.

"Thank you so much Nyrue. This ring means so much to me. For us to have gone through so much with my sister, yet you still thought about her. That means the world to me."

"I don't care about all that ma. As long as you are happy, all that other shit doesn't matter." I kissed the back of her hand as we rode home. We laid down and I held her close. I fell asleep with a smile branded on my face.

Chapter 22

Bree:

"Well, that shit failed again. I am done trying with these niggas. I wish you could physically tell me what to do because I am so lost. I'm thinking about moving to Miami and starting over. I can hear you now telling me that running from my problems won't solve anything, but it will help heal my broken heart. I heard Dakota is back with his other baby mama, which doesn't seem to surprise me. The boys are getting bigger every day and bad as hell." *Silence.*

"These are moments I feel like were stolen from you. I wasn't supposed to be here, at a cemetery, telling you about your nephews. You were supposed to be right here by my side, helping me raise them. I miss you so much, Adore, that it hurts. I know it may seem like life has gone on without you, but I'm just trying to keep pushing with no motivation. True enough, my sons are all the motivation I need, but I feel like I'm doing this with no backbone. I have nobody I can go to for guidance any more. Nobody that could shed an ounce of light on what I'm going through. I feel weak, sis. I'm all alone. I wish I was able to pick up the phone and call you so that I could just hear your voice once more. I guess it's just wishful thinking. I miss you and I want you to know that. Your life was taken when you barely got to live."

My shirt was soaked because the tears were constantly falling. I missed my sister more than anything. Nobody knew how I felt because I had such a hard exterior but, inside, I was breaking. The only other person that I felt loved me betrayed me by throwing a sledgehammer through my heart. I stood up and dusted myself off, preparing to leave. I had no feelings any more. My heart was frozen and damaged. There was nobody I could trust besides my kids. All I felt in my heart was the feeling of revenge. I didn't want to be that way, so I dropped back to my knees and prayed.

"Heavenly Father, I come to you as humble as I know how. Father, I come to you in need of guidance. The guidance to steer me back in the direction of love, guidance to show me that having malicious feelings in my heart is not your will. Father, I know that the thoughts roaming through my head are of evil and I ask that you help my wounds heal, Father. Father, I ask that you help fix my heart to forgive my sister's killer. I am a child of God and I know that a child of God would not cause harm to others. I come to you asking for forgiveness for even having such thoughts. Thank you, Father. In the name of Jesus, I pray, amen." I dusted off once again and started walking towards my car. As I got closer, I noticed someone was leaning against it. When I got closer, I couldn't believe my eyes. "Cortez."

"In the flesh."

"What are you doing in Atlanta?"

"I came to find the motherfucker that thought it would be okay to kill my baby girl. Now, I know me and Adore weren't on the best of terms, but she was still mine. Do you have any idea who did this?"

I attempted to shake my head no, but he cocked his head to the side. Cortez was Adore's ex-boyfriend and a crazy nigga he was. He took my sister through the pits of hell, but she loved his psychotic ass.

"Now, before you sit here and lie to me, you should think about it. You know me well enough to know that I did my homework before I boarded the plane to come here. You should also know that now that I'm here, I'm not leaving this muhfucka until that nigga is dead."

"Cortez, I-"

"You what? Don't sit here and say you don't know because you know exactly who it was, but I want to know why."

"A lot happened when she came here. You can't come here trying to kill anybody because it won't bring her back."

"Wasn't your lil simple ass just asking God to take ill feelings from your heart and some more bullshit? Fuck out of here yo."

"Why do you even care anyway? Y'all weren't even together."

"Me and Adore knew what was up. She had my heart and she knew it. She only moved here because I sent her here for her safety. Don't believe the hype from whatever she told you. I ended things with her to keep her alive. So, for my niggas here to tell me somebody killed her, that pissed me off. I don't know what reason she gave you for coming here and I really don't give a fuck, but I need to know everything you know about this nigga King." I shook my head no and he yanked me toward him by my shirt.

"Bree, please don't make this a big deal when it doesn't have to be." He took out his pistol and started rubbing it down the side of my face. A lone tear escaped my eyes as I thought that I would be welcoming death sooner than later. My heart was jumping out of my chest.

"Come on ma, give me what I need, so I can be on my way. I don't feel comfortable at this cemetery."

He pushed me back and I straightened myself out. "He has a club downtown on Peachtree. I wish you would let this go because he has a family and I don't want no parts of this."

"You got involved the day she was killed. You ain't shit, trying to save the nigga that took your sister's life from her." He got in his car and pulled off.

"What the hell did I just do?"

King:

"Why do it always take you forever to get dressed? Hurry the fuck up Dior."

"I'm coming Chance, damn. Patience is a virtue."

"Yeah yeah, hurry up."

My wife was the slowest at getting dressed and that shit irked a nigga's nerves. I brought her down to Ft. Lauderdale just to get away from the city for a few days, since we didn't get to go on our honeymoon. We were leaving tonight, so I planned on making the best of it. She finally came down the stairs and when I saw her, I could have sworn my heart stopped.

"Looking good baby. About damn time though."

"Blah, blah, blah. I have to perfect myself before I go anywhere. Are you ready?"

"I been ready for about an hour now."

"Whatever, let's go." We walked outside and got into the car. We headed to this steakhouse called Timpano. I pulled up and found us a parking space. We went inside and were immediately seated. After our food came, we sat and talked while we ate. We were having a good time and I was happy she was enjoying herself.

"Babe, I would love to live here. It's so beautiful."

"That's crazy because I was thinking the same shit. We can try that shit out and I go to Atlanta on the weekends to check on the club. This might surprise you, but I was thinking about letting your brother run it and see how everything checks out."

"Aww baby. I would love..." She froze before she could finish her sentence. It was like fear took over her body because her eyes were getting watery and her hands were shaking.

"Dior, what's wrong?"

"It's... it's... him."

"It's who?" She shook her head no. I looked into my wife's eyes and saw fear. I looked back over my shoulder and saw an older guy with a younger woman.

"Baby, what is it?" She wiped the tears that managed to escape her eyes.

"My father's friend, that's him." It took me a minute to register what she was saying but when I did, rage took over me. I felt the veins bulging out of the side of my neck. I was livid. No wonder I couldn't find this nigga because he had relocated in Ft. Lauderdale.

"I will be right back."

"Chance… wait. It's ok."

"Nah, fuck that. You didn't see the pain and fear that I saw when you saw him. Now, I will be back." I went outside to my car and got my 9mm. I screwed the silencer on it and tucked it behind my back. I went back inside and sat back down. I moved my seat closer to Dior so that I could watch his every move. A few minutes later, he got up and headed towards the bathroom. *Father, I repent for my sins. Please forgive me.* I looked around the restaurant and noticed there were no cameras inside.

"I got to piss, I'll be right back." I kissed her forehead and went to the bathroom. I walked in and stood against the sink until the nigga came out of the stall. He walked out and looked me up and down.

"What up man? You look familiar young blood."

181

Without responding, I pulled out my gun and put it in his mouth. I pushed him up against the wall and backed up with my 9 still pointed at him.

"Come on man. I don't have no money."

"Money? Nah, that ain't the issue. This is about my wife. I'm about to send you right there with your homie Roberto." His eyes widened and I shot him right in the mouth. I tucked my gun back on my waistline and went and sat back down like nothing happened.

"You alright?"

"Yeah, I had to shit."

"Oh ok. Well, I'm ready to go if you are." We got up and went back to the beach house. Dior packed our bags while I called my mother to check on the kids. Since Cali had moved out, she was always lonely, so she kept the kids for us. I couldn't wait for my sister to give birth to my niece or nephew. Dior came down and we headed to the field. We boarded the jet and headed back to our city. As soon as we touched down, Dior went to pick up the kids while I went to the club to make sure the weekend went by smooth. When I got there, all of the sections had been rented out and the club was damn near packed to capacity.

"What up Chub? I see this bitch moving tonight."

"Hell yeah boos. It's been lit all weekend. How was your trip?"

"It was a good one. Wifey enjoyed herself so that's all that matters."

"True shit. Be easy then boss."

He went back and stood at the door. Chub was a good friend. He started out just being my bouncer, but we built a friendship along the way. He was a cool cat. I walked through the club feeling like the man of the year as I made my way to my office. As usual, Ryan had my bottle of Cîroc sitting on my desk. I did my paperwork and took a look at all the sales I made over the weekend. This weekend alone, I had made over $85,000. A nigga was really living. I was writing down numbers when I heard the cock of a gun, then I looked up. I had never seen this nigga and couldn't understand why niggas felt this was the place to try and kill me. I had to laugh because he was just as dumb as Los.

"What up? Who you?"

"Shut up nigga. So, you the nigga King? Wow, your soft ass bodying muhfuckas?"

"Y'all niggas talk too damn much. Did you come to kill me or not because as you can see, I got shit to do."

"Fuck that. I'm sure Adore had shit to do too, but you didn't give a fuck."

"Oh, you came to kill me over some pussy? You getting revenge for a bitch that was dick crazy over the next nigga." I laughed while biting my lip. "I swear I can't take you niggas serious. So, what's up? Are you going to pull the trigger or nah because I'm not in the mood for another sad ass therapy session?"

"Fuck you." He cocked the gun and turned it to the side.

183

"You ain't getting no real money. You ain't scaring no motherfucking body. But you know what-"

"He got a rider." Dior shot him in the back of the head before he could even turn around.

Chapter 23

Dior:

I had the time of my life while we were in Ft. Lauderdale. Chance catered to me in ways I never knew that he could. It felt good to get away from the city and the kids, but I missed my babies. As soon as we landed, I jumped in the car and headed to Ms. Joyce house to get them. When I got there, Carson and Cayleigh were sleeping while Christian was up watching TV.

"So, how was trip?"

"I had a great time. I rode the jet skis on the beach and damn near drowned. You know my ass can't swim."

"What the hell you doing on them if you can't swim crazy?"

"I have always wanted to ride one. Your son was laughing his ass off while I was fighting with the water to let me live." Mama Joyce was cracking up. She poured us a shot and we made a toast.

"To new life." We each took our shots to the head and went into the living room. We sat down and chatted for a while until my phone rang.

"Hello?"

"Dior... Dior are you there?"

"Yeah, what's up Bree? Why do you sound like that?"

"You have to get to Chance. I did something that I really regret."

"Aubree, what the fuck are you talking about?"

"I know your husband killed my sister. I know it. Her ex-boyfriend is here to kill King and he will be at the club tonight. He made me tell him, Dior. I am so…" That was all I needed to know before I hung up. I would deal with that snitching ass bitch later but, for now, I had to get to my man.

"Mama Joyce, something is going on at the club and I need to get there. I will be right back." I rushed out of the house and peeled out on the way to the club.

"I can't believe this bitch gave a nigga info to kill my husband. Nobody fucks with my family and gets away with it." I pulled up to the club and sent Chance a text just to make sure everything was ok.

Hey babe, everything ok?

Hubby: Hell yeah. The club ate good while we were gone. I will be home within the next hour.

Ok.

Since he was texting back, I knew that ole boy had not made it yet. I pulled my car around to the front and let valet park it. I walked inside the club and found a table close to the stairs that led to Chance's office. I told Ryan to give me a shot of Tequila while I waited. After thirty minutes, I watched as a dark skinned dude walked past me and headed up the stairs. He blew a kiss at me and continued on his way. Once I saw him reach the top, I stood up and followed behind him. I saw him go into Chance's office, but I waited to enter. I stood outside of the door and listened to what was being said.

"Oh, you came to kill me over some pussy. You getting revenge for a bitch that was dick crazy over the next nigga. I swear, I can't take you niggas serious. So, what's up? Are you going to pull the trigger or nah because I'm not in the mood for another sad ass therapy session?"

"Fuck you." He cocked the gun and turned it to the side.

"You ain't getting no real money. You ain't scaring no motherfucking body. But, you know what…"

At that moment, I knew he was about to pull the trigger. I pulled my gun out quickly and cocked it. I stepped into the doorway behind him and said, "He got a rider." I shot him in the back of the head.

"Dior, what are you doing here? And where are my kids?"

"Bree called and told me he would be coming here. I will save the rest of the story for when we get home, but I will be paying that bitch a visit. The kids are still at your mother's. I was there when Bree called. I know you about to fuss at me for using the gun but I had to. There was no way I was about to lose you, not like that. You know mama got you." I pulled her into me and grabbed her ass. I started kissing her then turned her around, pulling down her pants. I pulled my pants down and pulled her panties to the side. I plunger my dick in her and started fucking her from the back.

"Mm, bab... y."

"I love you, girl."

"I love you too." I was showing her my appreciation in ways that she loved. I was addicted to this woman and everything about her. She started throwing her ass back as I gripped her hair.

"Fuck girl. Throw that ass back just like that."

"Mm, I'm cumin."

"Cream the dick then baby." Her juices poured down on my dick as I filled her tunnel up with my semen. I walked over and grabbed some napkins to clean us off.

"Now, go get my kids and get them to sleep. You got a long night ahead."

"Ok daddy."

Epilogue
One year later

Cody:

"Come on Jas. You have to push ma."

"I can't; it hurts too bad."

Jas was giving birth to my baby boy. I knew that she would end up pregnant, but I didn't mind. I loved the hell out of her and would give her all the babies in the world if I could. She made me a better nigga, no lie. Since we had been together, I had not cheated, not once. We had just gotten engaged last week and a nigga wouldn't have it any other way. Bree had up and left Atlanta and I had not heard from her in damn near a year. That shit fucked with a nigga daily. I never thought she would turn out to be one of those salty ass baby mamas, but her no neck ass did just that. The sad part about it was that she left the boys and never called to check on them. I prayed every single day that they didn't turn out like me. Luckily, they had Jas around so they had a mother figure because I didn't have that. I was now part owner of King's club and the money was flowing quite lovely. Jas had been a little fucked up because we had found out the nigga Los was dead. She went through a little grieving period where she didn't want to be bothered. I had officially gone legit and life couldn't be better. I had too many damn kids to keep running these streets and didn't want to end up dead or in jail and miss out on any parts of their life. I had come to the realization that my problems with women was because I lacked the love from my mother, but I didn't want that to hinder me anymore. I didn't want to go about life hurting women and end up alone. Jas was more than my woman; she was my best friend. Club Paradise was also making money and I was happy about that. Me and Dior had gotten a little closer with Moe this past year and she wasn't that bad. I apologized to her for giving her such a hard time.

"Ok dad, we need you to stand here while she makes this last push. Mommy, on the next contraction, I want you to give me one more big push."

She nodded her head and waited. I was excited that my little man was about to enter this world. She started pushing as the doctor counted to ten. Loud cries filled the room as my lil nigga made his grand entrance. I got the scissors and cut the cord. He weighed 9lbs and 11oz and he was 20 inches long. He was identical to me, except he had Jas' chocolate complexion.

"I want to hold him."

I fell in love all over again at that moment when Dakota Jr. entered the world. Me and King had finally become closer and he was a cool dude. We really didn't have a choice because Dior wasn't having it any other way. I had even gotten a lil closer with his sister's boyfriend, Rue. We had a plan to open up another club down in Miami where he was from. This would be the start of something new.

Jas:

I would have never thought I would give birth to another baby but fucking with Dakota and his super sperm would always get you there. We had been going strong this past year and I loved it. This relationship was everything that I dreamed it would be. He had done a 360 and changed all of his ways. I didn't have trust issues or nothing when it came to him. We were now engaged and I couldn't wait to become his wife. Our family was complete. Since we had the boys, things were much better than before because Demi was more than happy to be with her brothers every day. She was almost 2 years old and the twins were going on 3. Me and Dior still did our weekend play dates and all the kids loved it. Them growing up together was such a blessing. When I found out Los had been murdered, a piece of me left with him. We had some great times so, of course, it hurt me. We had grown feelings for one another, but that was of the past. I now had my baby boy and from this moment forward, I would focus on my family.

"I love you, Dakota."

"I love you too, Jas. I swear, I got you and my kids for whatever." He kissed my forehead and, at that moment, I felt secure.

King:

"Come on big girl."

"Shut the hell up."

Dior was pregnant again with another baby girl. I had the perfect package, 2 girls and 2 boys. Unfortunately for her, I wanted one more. We had recently moved to Fairburn into a 7-bedroom mansion that I had got built. Our front yard was seven acres and I loved that shit. I still had my club, but I wasn't really running it. Dakota had taken over majority of the responsibilities of it. Me and that nigga had finally squashed whatever beef we had. He was alright, but that nigga's mouth was ruthless. He was one nigga that had no filter. Shit crazy how life had turned out for all of us, but life was wonderful. I had everything I wanted, but I still missed my little sister. Cali and my mother were doing ok for the most part, taking shit a day at a time. Moe was coming around more often and spending more time with Christian. She had agreed to let us keep Christian for a while longer until she was completely on her feet. Our one-year anniversary was in a few days and I had the surprise of a lifetime for my wife. What can I say? I had no complaints. This not the last y'all will ever hear of me. King Chance shall return bih.

Dior:

Well y'all, my extra fertile ass knocked up once again and I am so over it. This little girl was taking me through hell and I was ready for her little ass to come. I was only 6 months but felt like I was at the end of the road. Things with me and Chance was more than perfect and I was looking forward to a lifetime with him. The kids were getting bigger and were more spoiled than ever. Christian was turning 6 next week. Cayleigh was 2 and Carson was turning 1 tomorrow. Chance thought in his head that he was getting one more out of me, but this was it. I had already secretly signed my papers to have my tubes tied. Jas had just given birth to my nephew and I was so anxious to see him. It took me some time to get over it, but I was actually happy for them. They actually complimented each other pretty well. I couldn't wait to be the matron of honor in their wedding and see the same smile that I had, on her face.

Moe and I were getting back close and, I must say, I enjoyed it. I had even grown a bond with my aunt Carole and her grandmother. We eventually told them that we were behind Roberto's murder but after telling them about his past, they let go of the anger. We still had Christian for the time being, but I knew, eventually, we would have to give her back custody. I had grown so attached to him but, at the end of the day, she was still his mother. A part of me wanted to search for the guy that was responsible for my mother's murder, but I was just over the drama. I was finally happy and at peace, so I decided to let it go, as long as he didn't come for my brother. All of the kids were being raised together though and that's all that mattered. Nobody had heard from Bree and I couldn't wait to catch up with that bitch. So, if y'all hear from her, tell her that Dior said, "Get at me." Life had been much better ever since I fell in love with the wrong thug. He turned out to be just right for me.

Rue:

I was now a father and the feeling was unexplainable. My baby girl was the most beautiful thing I had ever laid eyes on. She was the exact replica of her mother. She was Cali from the head to her little feet. Her eyes were the exact same color and she had a head full of hair. The past 2 months had been wonderful as I transitioned from not only a real man but a father. There was nothing on this earth that could take me away from them, except for the man above. We were now planning a wedding and I knew she was about to empty my pockets. I didn't mind at all though, as long as I had her. She still had her moments where she broke down thinking about Chasity, but I made sure to remain by her side. Me, King, and Dakota had finally got out shit together. We were planning something special for the ladies and I was excited. Mama Joyce was keeping all the kids, so we were about to turn up. We had also started on a project down in Miami, a new club. That was in the process of getting built. Next time y'all hear from me, I will be a married man and I will be richer than ever.

Moe:

I was so blessed to have my mother and sister back in my life. I had even gotten close with my grandmother, even though she was the reason my mother got rid of me in the first place. Life had been a walk in the park for me ever since and I wouldn't trade it. I also had Christian from time to time and that was enough. Me and Dior had become the best of friends again and it felt good. She even trusted me enough to be around Chance alone, so I knew we were good. I guess she knew it was completely between us. Me and Dakota were good too, but he still was an asshole. I don't think that would ever change. I had been dealing with this guy named Pain and he was quite the charmer. I know I will be back, so I was willing to see where this thing with him goes.

Cali:

It had been a year since I saw my father and a part of me didn't care. After he left that day, I realized that I was probably better off without him. I didn't blame my mother because I realized she was only protecting me. We had gotten much closer since Chastity passed. "She is so beautiful sis and I wish you could have met her. Sometimes, when she stares at the ceiling and laughs, I get a feeling that it's you playing with her. You know how they say that babies see angels? You probably wouldn't care but me and Nyrue are getting married soon. I am so happy sis. I feel so complete. The only thing that's missing is you. Mommy stays home more now. I slick think she got out of the game. She stays home now and watches all of the kids. I love you Chas and I miss you. Next time, I will bring Ny'ree to see you. Until next time sis." I came by the cemetery every Saturday to visit Chastity. Even though it had been a year and a half since she left, I still hadn't healed from the pain of her being gone. I had my baby girl and she was my biggest blessing. Nyrue was such a great father and fiancé. He would sit home and watch her once a week so that I could have a girl's day and pamper myself. I didn't need more than that because I knew bills had to be paid and he didn't want me to work. Dior had it rough because she was helping both me and Jas plan our weddings. Them and Moe had become the sisters that I never had and I enjoyed hanging with them. Dior had my brother in check and it was so funny to me because I had never seen him act the way that he did with her. I guess it's true what they say; when you meet your match, it always gets you right.

Bree:

"Yes baby, fuck me right there." He slapped me on my ass as he plunged in and out from the back. The pleasure he was giving my body was something you couldn't imagine.

"Fuck girl. You wet as fuck." I reached under me and massaged his balls.

"I'm about to cum."

"Me too. Come on." We released our fluids in unison and I fell forward. Now, I know y'all probably hate me, but I don't give a fuck. I had to do what I had to do. After the whole ordeal with Cortez, I moved out of Atlanta. It just wasn't for me anymore. I was also still hurt that Dakota got with Jas after he cheated. I was so hurt that I never wanted to see him again. I moved out of Atlanta but left my boys back home. I knew I would catch hell with Dakota if I took them, so I left. I hadn't spoken with him since then and I missed my boys so much. Don't think that I'm a bad mother, but I was going back for them when I got myself together here. I was now living in New Jersey and I loved it. I had met this guy 6 months ago named Blue and he was the connect. Talk about a nigga with money, he had plenty of it. Blue helped me through the pain that I felt each day, once I realized I had no one. He had become my best friend. I was going to get my boys soon and love them the way a mother should. Jasmine could never be there mother, no matter how hard she tried. Y'all be easy until we meet again.

The End

Products of A Thug: 18 years later

(Sneak peek)

Christian:

Deimo and Demarri were supposed to be coming over to chill with these lil broads from the club the other night. I knew Deimo wasn't making no noise though because he was faithful today. He was the only nigga I knew that was faithful every day, except for Wednesday. Who did shit like that? He said Wednesdays were his free day but, regardless, cheating was cheating. Those were the two most throwed off twins I had ever met, but Uncle Cody raised them like that. I heard music thumping from down the street and I knew thing 1 and thing 2 were here. They pulled in and the females pulled in behind them. My sister Cayleigh and my cousin Ny'Ree walked up, and I knew they were probably about to start that hating shit.

"Shaking my damn head. Y'all niggas nasty as fuck. It's always different females coming over here. I don't see what they be seeing in y'all ugly asses."

"Girl, stop hating with your lonely ass. You just mad; ain't nobody checking for you." Demarri and Cayleigh never got along because they were just alike. Cayleigh was a petty ass female and he hated it. He only hated it because he felt like he was supposed to be the only petty one out of the bunch. He waved Cayleigh off and came into the house. Her and Ny'Ree sat on the porch and sparked up a blunt.

"What up pretty ass nigga?"

"Chill out with all that. What up Doublemint twins?" We dapped each other up and I moved over so that they could come in. Demarri came straight in with a blunt in his mouth.

"Aye man, your sister a hater. No wonder Demi don't be fucking with her ass."

"Watch out with all that lame shit nigga. Demi just be thottin around the city, so she can't have time to hang with nobody."

"Nigga, I will kill you about my sister and you know that, so hold your tongue."

"Whatever nigga; don't talk that shit about my sister then." I wasn't lying though. Demi was hot in the ass. Every baller in the city knew who she was and I hated that shit. I loved my little cousin since I was the oldest out of everybody, but her ass needed to chill.

The broads from the club went and sat down beside them and the chick I was fucking with grabbed my hand and led me to the back room. I knew it. I knew when I saw her at the club that she was a thot. Thot was written on her forehead and her whole persona screamed thot.

"Straight like that huh? You pull up and go straight to the bedroom, no talking?"

"I don't have time to play games. We grown, right?"

"Hell yeah. Aye pretty ass niggas, I'll be back."

"Shut up nigga. I hope you got a rubber."

"I keep rubbers nigga." Deimo looked at his brother and smacked his teeth.

"You got some nerve to talk about safe sex when your hoe ass done had hoes fake being pregnant on your ass five times. If you were wearing a rubber, you would have never believed that so you can't give nobody advice."

"Shut up man, who asked you?"

Demarri was a real life male whore. That nigga never fucked the same female twice and that shit was disgusting. He was also the petty one. He was my uncle Cody all the way. I walked to the back and closed the door. Shorty wasted no time getting on her knees. When she took me in her mouth, I couldn't help but notice how loose her throat was. How does that work?

"Aye ma stop, JUST STOP!"

"What's wrong?"

"You. You literally have a deep throat. It's too deep baby girl and I can't get with it." She stood up, like she was about to try and protest, when I heard arguing coming from the front room. *This nigga.* it wouldn't take a rocket scientist to know that it was Demarri in the front, probably arguing with one of these females because he had a smart ass mouth.

"Girl, I will have my sister beat your ass, so I suggest you back your invisible edges having ass up. I don't like calling females out of their name but you pushing it."

"Yo Marri, what the fuck your dumb ass doing now man damn?"

"Cuz, she mad at me because I called her ass out. She took her lil Cinderella shoes off and had Beauty and the Beast feet. Her big toe running away from the rest of them muhfuckas. The big toe sit at a 90-degree angle and look like it's ready to scream, action." Everybody was laughing and I rubbed my hand down my face. I swear, he had no fucking sense.

She stood up and pointed at him. "He is a rude ass nigga and niggas like him get dealt with in these streets."

Me, Deimo, and Demarri got in her space, but Deimo was directly in front of her.

"Bitch, I know you not threatening my brother?"

"Nah, for real."

"I didn't mean it like that."

Her home girls pulled on our shirts, but we weren't budging. "You better learn how to choose better words baby girl. We don't take threats lightly and neither will our sisters, if we told them."

Luckily, my sister and Ny'Ree had already left or it would have been a serious problem.

"Now, I suggest you, loose throat, and missing edges get the fuck out."

"Wait what? I have edges and my throat not loose."

"I can't tell. It looks to me like they been kidnapped, now get the fuck out."

"And you a damn lie. Your throat loose as hell. I would hate to have fucked because I know that shit wide open." Demarri's phone started ringing and he stepped in the kitchen to answer it. Since his phone was damn near non-existent, he could only hear it on speakerphone.

"YO...WHO THIS?"

"MARRI HELP ME."

"DEMI!"

Coming Soon...